The Usborne
Illustrated
Tales of
King
Arthur

The Usborne Illustrated Tales of King Arthur

Retold by Sarah Courtauld

Illustrated by Natasha Kuricheva

Contents

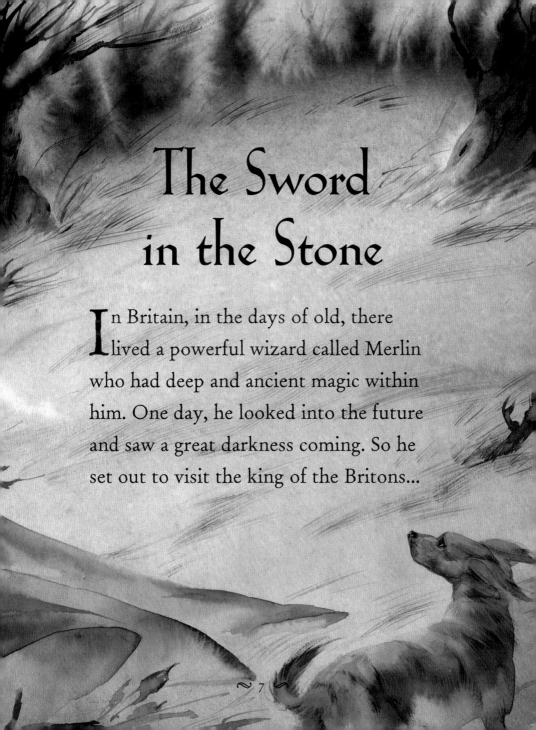

The Sword in the Stone

I n Britain, in the days of old, there lived a powerful wizard called Merlin who had deep and ancient magic within him. One day, he looked into the future and saw a great darkness coming. So he set out to visit the king of the Britons...

The king's name was Uther Pendragon, and
he ruled the southern parts of Britain. For the
moment, the lands he ruled were at peace. But
Merlin had dark tidings for the king.

He found Uther at Tintagel, an enchanted
castle in Cornwall. There he told the surprised
king, "Soon you will have a son, a son destined
for greatness. But, before two years have passed,
you will die. If anyone knows of his existence,
the child will be killed in the struggle for power
after your death. The very hour the baby is born,
you must deliver him to me, and never speak of
him again. I will make sure he is safe until his
time comes."

Uther could not bear the thought that any
child of his might come to harm, and so he
agreed.

On the night the baby was born, Merlin carried him away under the cover of darkness. No one had any idea what became of him.

After this, everything happened just as Merlin had predicted. Within two years, Uther was dead and his knights were fighting one another over who would take the throne. Soon, unrest spread throughout the land. Outlaws roamed the countryside, and everywhere there was looting, squabbling and uncertainty.

All the while, Merlin waited. At last, when the time was right, he set out to see the archbishop in London. He told him if he called a great gathering of knights on Christmas Day, the true-born King of all Britain would be found.

That Christmas Day, the cathedral was packed with knights. The service had just begun, when there was a tremendous thump outside the church. Everyone rushed outside. A giant slab of stone had appeared, as if it had fallen from the sky. Jutting out of the stone was a long, gleaming silver sword. Enscribed on the stone itself were the words:

WHOEVER PULLS THE SWORD
FROM THIS STONE
WILL BE THE RIGHTFUL KING
OF ALL BRITAIN

The archbishop sent the knights inside. But when the service was over, they hurried back out to the churchyard. One by one, they heaved at the hilt, but the sword was stuck fast.

"It seems the King of all Britain is not yet

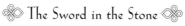

'A giant slab of stone had appeared, as if it had fallen from the sky.'

here," the archbishop declared. "But he will come in time. Let messengers be sent throughout Britain, telling of this marvel. All knights who wish to try the sword should come to a grand tournament on New Year's Day, here in London."

New Year's Day came, and the streets of London were thronging with knights on their way to the tournament. One of them was Sir Ector, who was riding with his son, Sir Kay, and Kay's younger brother, Arthur.

Kay was in a hurry. It was his first tournament and he was determined to make his father proud. He was just imagining how he was going to defeat all of the older knights, when he had a horrible thought…"Stop!" he shouted, pulling on his reins. "I've left my sword at the inn! Arthur, fetch it! Go!"

"At once," Arthur replied. He spurred his horse and galloped away. But when he got to the inn, the doors were locked. Every last person had gone to see the tournament. Suddenly, he remembered the sword he'd glimpsed earlier that day, jutting out of a stone slab in the cathedral churchyard.

"I'll take that sword," he thought, knowing nothing of its significance. "It's not doing anyone any use in the churchyard. Kay will not be without a sword today!"

So he galloped as fast as he could to the empty churchyard, pulled the sword from the stone and raced off to the tournament.

When he arrived, he weaved through the crowds until he found Kay, and presented him with the sword.

"That's not mine," Kay said, and then his eyes widened as he recognized the sword. He had watched several knights try to pull it from the stone that very morning, while Arthur had been busy arranging lodgings. Kay seized the sword and rushed to find Sir Ector.

"Father – look!" he said excitedly.

"What is it?" said Sir Ector.

"I have the sword from the stone, Father! That must mean that I am the rightful King of all Britain!"

"Did you pull it out yourself?" Sir Ector asked, looking hard at his son.

"Yes," Kay replied.

"You swear that is the truth?" Ector asked.

"I, I— Arthur brought it to me," Kay confessed, his cheeks burning with shame. So Sir Ector called Arthur to him and made him explain exactly what had happened. When he heard Arthur's tale, he took Kay and Arthur straight to the churchyard.

There, he thrust the sword back into the stone. He and Sir Kay tried to pull it out, but it was stuck fast as if it had been lodged there for a thousand years. "Try it again," Sir Ector ordered Arthur. Arthur took hold of the hilt, and the blade slid out easily.

Sir Ector bowed his head and knelt down before Arthur in the snow. Sir Kay gaped at Arthur and then hurriedly did the same.

"What? What are you doing?" asked Arthur.

"I love you as if you were my own son," Sir Ector said gently. "But it is time to tell you, Arthur: you are not of my blood. One night, when you were a baby, the wizard Merlin brought you to my house in secret. He made me promise to keep you safe and raise you as my own child. I have done so gladly."

"So... you are not my father?" Arthur said, struggling to hold back his tears.

"Arthur," Sir Ector said quietly, "whoever draws this sword is the rightful King of all Britain. Your destiny lies beyond our family."

Arthur's head was spinning. "If I am to be king, I hope I never fail you," he managed to say.

"Sir Kay and I swear loyalty to you, our king, for all our days," said Sir Ector.

Sir Ector went straight to the archbishop and

told him all that had happened. The archbishop made an official announcement to all the knights and noblemen who had come to the tournament.

The news was greeted with roars of laughter. Nobody believed that a boy who was not yet even a knight could possibly be the true king. They would not even let him try to prove it.

"If nobody else has been found, your boy can come back at Pentecost and try again," the archbishop told Sir Ector. The sword was thrust back into the stone and word was sent out for more barons, lords, knights and kings to try their hand before Pentecost. Many tried, but not one of them could prise the sword from the stone.

At the feast of Pentecost, a huge crowd was watching when Arthur walked up to the sword once more and put his hand on its hilt. From the

shadows, Merlin was watching too. In front of
everyone, Arthur drew the sword from the stone
and lifted the shining blade into the air.

There was a hush, before people in the crowd
started shouting: "The sword has spoken!
Arthur! Arthur! Arthur is our king!"

Soon the whole crowd was chanting with one
voice, and suddenly they all kneeled before
Arthur. Then Arthur kneeled, and the
Archbishop took the sword and knighted him.

That same day, Arthur was
crowned in the cathedral. He
looked out across the sea
of expectant faces and
felt his courage grow
strong within him. "I
vow to bring justice and

peace to this land. I will drive out invaders and right the wrongs of my people," he declared.

When the service ended, Arthur walked out onto the steps of the cathedral to be greeted by a deafening cheer from the crowd. For a moment he reeled, gripped by a sudden fear of all that lay ahead, but then he became aware of a tall, cloaked figure standing beside him.

"Do not be afraid," said the man. "I have seen your destiny, and it is as bright as the evening star. Greatness awaits you, Arthur, and I will be here to guide you."

It was only then that Arthur realized the man beside him must be the wizard Merlin. And all his fear left him as they walked down the steps together into the brilliant sunshine.

The First Battle

Arthur chose the city of Camelot for his capital and, at first, his presence brought a lull of peace. But the kings who ruled other parts of Britain were jealous of this unknown boy, the supposed King of all Britain, and they sent him a message. "We are coming to put you in your proper place. Be ready for us."

When Merlin heard this, he led Arthur into Camelot's strongest castle tower and asked his most loyal knights to protect him. Before long, the hostile kings and hundreds of knights had surrounded the castle, and were baying for Arthur's blood.

After two weeks, Merlin came out of the castle. The kings and knights started yelling at once: "Why is this beardless *boy* called King of all Britain? Why should we bow to him?"

"He'll never rule us!"

"He's a child! He's never fought in his life!"

"Silence, all of you!" Merlin thundered. "Listen, and I will tell you wondrous things."

A hush descended on the crowd as the great wizard spoke in his calm, clear voice. "The darkness that surrounds these lands is greater than all of you and will consume you unless you heed my words. I have seen a shining path through the darkness, and Arthur is the one to lead the way along it.

"Even now, in the enchanted Isle of Avalon, where magic dwells, the wondrous sword Excalibur is waiting for its true owner, Arthur. With this sword, Arthur will do many great deeds.

"Arthur, only son of the great King Uther Pendragon, is your rightful king. He will be the best knight and the greatest ruler this realm has ever known. He will be good, generous, and just. He shall make this kingdom truly great, for a time, before darkness rules again."

When Merlin finished speaking, the crowd remained silent. Many knights were won over by the wizard's words. They fell to their knees and vowed their allegiance to Arthur.

But others dismissed Merlin as a dreamer. As the gaunt figure disappeared back inside the tower, they whispered among themselves. "Why should we listen to him? Leave him to his spells," they said. "He's meddling in something he doesn't understand."

Inside the tower, Merlin told Arthur what had happened. "The time for battle has come," he said. "There are now many more knights who will fight on your side. But you have no choice. You must fight your enemies. But do not be afraid, for they will never defeat you. Not even if they had ten times as many men!"

And so, the next morning, Merlin helped Arthur into his armour. And, although Arthur had never fought in battle, and he knew his men were outnumbered, he had faith that Merlin was right. He mounted his horse, ready to enter his first battle.

"Arthur, you must fight with good spirit," Merlin said. "But listen to me: fight with your old sword. Do not use the sword you pulled from the stone. Not until you feel the battle is lost."

With Merlin's words ringing in his ears, Arthur charged out of the castle, his loyal knights beside him. He flung himself into battle not like a boy, as his enemies had expected, but like a fearless lion.

His opponents fell back in surprise, but they soon rose up again. Wave after wave of soldiers rushed at him, and his knights fell by the dozen.

'He held it up and the light flooded the sky,
piercing the clouds with its brilliance.'

Then, as Arthur struggled on against the tide of enemies, a spear flew and knocked him from his horse. He looked up to see a knight looming over him, ready to strike. "All is lost," he thought. Then Merlin's words flashed into his mind, and he reached for the sword that had come from the stone.

As he drew it, the blade glowed with a bright, golden light. He held it up and the light flooded the sky, piercing the clouds with its brilliance. Men on all sides drew back, terrified, as Arthur jumped back into his saddle and charged, the power of the sword surging into him. As light faded from the blade, so Arthur's power grew.

Knights fled before his sword and, by nightfall, his enemies had all surrendered. King Arthur's first battle was won.

Excalibur

Soon afterwards, Arthur was seated in his Great Hall at Camelot. "I will bring peace to this land," he announced. "And if any of my subjects are in trouble, let them come to me and I will right their wrongs."

Just as he spoke these words, a young man burst into the hall...

"Give me vengeance, I beg you!" he said to Arthur. "Outside in the courtyard lies the body of a noble knight, Sir Miles. He was killed in a forest not far from here by a cruel knight called Sir Pellinore. This fiend lives in a golden pavilion and fights every knight who passes by. I beg you, bury my master and avenge his death!"

At this, a young squire called Gryflet came forward. "King Arthur, let me go!" he blurted. "Make me a knight so I may fight Sir Pellinore."

Gryflet was the same age as Arthur. The king considered that for a moment, then said, "You're not old enough or strong enough to fight such a knight."

"I beg you, let me prove my worth!" Gryflet pleaded. Before Arthur could reply, Merlin was beside him, whispering in his ear: "One day

Gryflet will make a great warrior. Do not let him fight today. Pellinore is the strongest knight in the land. He will certainly defeat him."

But Arthur could see the courage shining in Gryflet's eyes. "I will make you a knight," he said, "but promise me only to joust; do not fight Sir Pellinore on foot. And when you have fought him, return to me straight away."

"I promise," Gryflet replied. And so Arthur knighted him, and straight away Gryflet rode into the forest, searching for Sir Pellinore.

Before long, he spotted the golden pavilion, with a black horse standing beside it. In front of the pavilion was a large, brightly painted shield. Gryflet struck the shield so hard that it crashed to the ground and Sir Pellinore came tearing out of the pavilion, looking as strong as a bear.

"Why did you strike my shield? What do you want?" Sir Pellinore barked.

"To joust with you!" shouted Gryflet.

"You? Ha! You're a mere boy."

"Still, I wish to joust with you," Gryflet repeated.

"If you want to throw away your life, I'm not going to stop you," Sir Pellinore snarled, leaping up onto his horse.

So Gryflet and Sir Pellinore rode away from each other, turned and charged. Sir Gryflet struck Sir Pellinore's shield, and it shattered. But Sir Pellinore's lance had pierced Gryflet's side and he fell to the ground. Sir Pellinore jumped down from his horse and bent down over the young man. "If he lives, he'll make a fine knight one day," he thought. Then he picked him up and threw him across his horse. The steed galloped off through the forest and made its way back to Camelot.

Arthur had been watching all afternoon for Gryflet's return. When he saw the horse with Gryflet lying across the saddle, sorely wounded, he was furious with himself. "I should never have let him go," he thought. "Sir Pellinore must be stopped!" He set off at once, thundering through the forest to find Sir Pellinore.

But as he rode through the woods, he came across Merlin, being attacked by three robbers. "Flee, cowards!" Arthur yelled, drawing his sword. The thieves scattered before him as he rushed to Merlin's side.

"Merlin!" said Arthur. "For all your magic, you would have died if I hadn't been here!"

"No, Arthur," said Merlin quietly. "It is you who rides close to your death. Beware Sir Pellinore's strength and your own pride."

But Arthur shook off Merlin's strange words and rode on until he came to the pavilion and the huge, burly knight standing beside it.

"Why do you fight all the knights that come your way?" he asked.

"It is my custom," Sir Pellinore replied. "Any man tries to stop me at his peril."

"I will stop you!" said Arthur angrily.

"And I will defend my custom," Sir Pellinore replied, picking up his lance.

They rode at each other at full tilt, and each struck the other so hard that their lances shattered and both men crashed to the ground.

For a moment they were both dazed. Then

they sprang to their feet, drawing their swords.
Each hacked at the other's armour until it was
cut to pieces and the ground was stained with
blood.

At nightfall, they rested. Arthur groaned,
weak from his wounds. But he
was determined to win. He
thought of Gryflet lying
injured at Camelot
and struggled to his feet.
"Let us fight to the
end!" he roared.

"With pleasure," Sir
Pellinore snarled. Then Arthur swiped at Sir
Pellinore with all his strength. But as he did, his
sword broke in two. He was left holding the
useless hilt in his hand.

"Ha! Now you are in my power!" hissed Sir Pellinore. "Die or yield."

"Death is one thing," said Arthur proudly. "But to yield – never!"

He threw himself at Sir Pellinore and wrestled him to the ground. But in another moment Sir Pellinore had wrenched off Arthur's helmet and stood over him, the tip of his blade pressed to Arthur's bare neck.

"Now I'll have your head!" Sir Pellinore roared. But, just as he drew back his sword to strike, his eyes rolled back in his head. He stumbled backwards and sank to the ground.

Gasping, Arthur scrambled to his feet and saw Merlin standing behind Sir Pellinore's limp body. "What did you do?" Arthur demanded. "Is he dead? I would not have you kill him!"

"Hush," said Merlin. "Sir Pellinore is not dead. Although *you* would have been, had I not been here to save you."

He helped Arthur up onto his horse. "Sir Pellinore is merely sleeping. In time he will awake. One day he will serve you. Now, come with me."

Merlin led Arthur to a hermitage, deep in the forest, where an old man tended to his wounds. In three days he was healed.

"Now you are ready to return to Camelot," Merlin told him.

"I am ashamed," Arthur replied sadly, "for I have no sword."

"Do not worry," said Merlin. "Follow me."

He led Arthur into the forest. Deeper and deeper they rode, along secret pathways, until at last a wide valley opened up before them. In the valley was a clear blue lake. The whole scene was still and silent, and it felt to Arthur as if the air was thick with unseen spells. "What is this place?" he whispered, half afraid to speak.

"Beyond the lake is the enchanted Isle of Avalon, which is full of spirits," Merlin told him. "Now, behold your sword."

Arthur gazed across the water and saw a pale arm stretching out of the lake, holding a sword with a richly jewelled scabbard. Beyond it, a woman dressed all in white was walking across the water towards him.

"Welcome, Sire," she said gently, when she reached his side. "I am the Lady of the Lake. That sword is Excalibur. Do you wish to take it as your sword and wear it?"

❧ Excalibur ❧

'Arthur gazed across the water and saw a pale arm
stretching out of the lake, holding a sword...'

"I do," said Arthur.

"The sword shall be yours, in exchange for one gift," the Lady continued.

"Tell me, and it shall be yours," said Arthur. Then he watched as a ship appeared and floated across the water towards him. "Step into the ship," said the Lady. "I shall ask for the gift when the time comes."

Arthur climbed on board the ship and it began to glide across the water, as if guided by magic. When he reached the sword, he clasped the hilt, and at once the hand disappeared beneath the surface and was seen no more.

On their way back through the forest, Arthur was silent, overwhelmed by everything he'd seen. "Which do you think is stronger, the sword or the scabbard?" Merlin asked him, with the hint of a smile on his face.

"The sword, of course," Arthur replied.

"Once more, you are wrong," said Merlin. "The sword is full of a deep and powerful magic, but the scabbard is more powerful still. While you have this scabbard with you, you will never lose a drop of blood."

When Arthur returned home, he showed Excalibur to his knights and told them of his fight against Sir Pellinore. Some of Arthur's knights wondered why Arthur had risked his own his life to fight the dreaded knight. Others were glad to serve such a king, who was as brave as his warriors.

Balyn and Balan

One day, a maiden arrived at
Camelot and begged for Arthur's
help. As she stood before him, she parted
her cloak to reveal an ornately jewelled
sword hanging from her belt.

43

"Why do you wear that sword, fair Lady?" asked Arthur.

"This sword is a token of my grief," she replied. "I shall not be free from it until I find a true and virtuous knight who can draw it from its scabbard."

"I may not be the bravest knight here, but let me try," said Arthur. He put his hand to the hilt and heaved, but the sword wouldn't budge.

"The right man will be able to pull it out easily," the maiden said. "But he must be a virtuous knight, with no evil in his heart."

So Arthur called to his men. "Come, brave knights! Let's see you test your virtue."

One by one, Arthur's knights tried to draw the sword, but no one could. When the last knight had failed, the maiden put her face in her hands and wept. "I thought that here at Camelot, I would find at least one man with a heart pure enough to draw it," she sobbed.

"I am truly sorry," Arthur said softly. "My knights are good men, but they are not destined to help you."

As he said this, a young knight called Balyn came forward. No one had thought of asking Balyn to draw the sword. He had been in prison for killing a cousin of King Arthur's. He was dressed in mud-spattered rags, and he hadn't dared ask to draw the sword, although he was sure in his heart that he could do it. But as the maiden turned to leave he blurted out: "Maiden, let me try to draw it! I know you may look at me and see only a poor knight, but fine clothes do not make an honest man."

The maiden stopped and looked at him.
"You speak wisely," she said. "Please, try to
draw the sword."

So Balyn took hold of the hilt, and pulled the
sword out easily. The whole court looked on,
astonished. The other knights started muttering,
jealous of Balyn's success. But the maiden
silenced them: "Here is a true, noble knight, the
best in the land," she said.

"Many are the wondrous
deeds that he will do. But
now, good knight – give
me back my sword."

Balyn stared at her
strangely, his eyes
burning with a sudden
fire. "I cannot!" he said.

The sword hummed in his hand, almost as if it were alive, and he felt its power flooding through his arm into his whole body. He suddenly felt sure of one thing – that this sword was destined for him, and him alone.

"You are making a great mistake," said the maiden. "And I am sorry for your sake, not mine. This is an enchanted sword, which the Lady of the Isle of Avalon gave to me. The weapon holds a dark and terrible magic within it. I ask you once more: please give me my sword."

But the longer Balyn held the sword, the more certain he felt that some great destiny lay before him. If he gave the sword back now he would be lost. His fist tightened around the hilt. "I'll take my chances," Balyn said. "But I can never give up this sword!"

"Listen to her, Balyn," Arthur commanded. "The sword is not yours."

"Return it to me," the maiden pleaded, "or with it you will slay your dearest friend. The sword is full of darkness. It will destroy you!"

"I will not," Balyn said. And no matter how much the maiden pleaded, he refused to give it up. As she left the court, her face pale with anguish, Balyn held the sword up to the light and gazed at it as if it were a precious jewel.

Then everyone fell silent, and Balyn turned to see the Lady of the Lake kneeling before Arthur.

"Sire," she said softly, "Not long ago, I

gave you Excalibur, and you promised me a gift
in return. I have come to claim it now."

Arthur nodded. "Of course, fair lady. You
may ask anything. What would you have?"

"The head of the knight who won the sword
today," she replied.

"Truly, I cannot give you that!" Arthur said.
"I would have no honour if I granted it! Sir
Balyn is my guest. Please, ask for any other gift."

"I will take nothing else," the Lady of the
Lake replied calmly. "You made a vow, and now
you must keep it."

Balyn strode up to the Lady of the Lake, his
eyes blazing. "Evil woman!" he cried. "You
would have my head?"

"I would," she said.

"Then you shall lose yours instead!" Balyn

yelled. And he lunged forward and sliced off the Lady's head. Her body slid to the floor.

"For shame!" Arthur thundered. "Balyn, you have disgraced me, and all my court! Be gone from this court forever."

"Sire, I have done no wrong!" Balyn shouted back. "She was a sorceress! She enchanted men and women – she wanted me dead!"

King Arthur looked coldly at Balyn. "You have done a disgraceful thing," he said. "Be gone from my court and from this kingdom. Never return unless, by some long penance or brave deed, you redeem your honour."

Balyn sheathed the sword and stormed out of the Hall. But as he galloped away from the court, his anger began to fade. He thought of Arthur's words and felt ashamed of what he had done. He

brought his horse to a halt and burst into tears.
"I will earn Arthur's forgiveness," he thought.
"But how?" He remembered that Arthur had a
deadly enemy called King Rience, a rebel who
was fighting to destroy him. He kicked his horse
into a gallop. "I will capture King Rience. Then
one day, Arthur will forgive me."

In Camelot, the knights were all talking about
Balyn and the terrible deed he had done.
Eventually one young knight, Sir Lanceour,
spoke out. "Justice must be done," he said.
"King Arthur, give me leave to follow Balyn
and kill him."

"You have my leave," Arthur said sadly.

So Lanceour put his spurs to his horse, and
rode through hills and valleys in search of the
disgraced knight.

Meanwhile, Merlin arrived at Camelot. When Arthur told him what had happened, Merlin's face grew grave.

"Evil has come to Camelot," he said quietly, "and greater evil shall follow. The sword was full of darkness and in the wrong hands it will reap only death. Balyn is not strong enough to wield that sword without it destroying him."

"Is there nothing you can do?" Arthur asked, but Merlin shook his head sadly. "One day the sword will bring a blessing to the kingdom. It will find its true owner in Galahad, the best of your knights. But before that day, Balyn will go to his death. He who would have been one of your best men."

"You cannot save him?" asked Arthur.

"I fear not," he said. "But I will follow him,

and see if there is any good I can bring him."

Deep in a forest, far from Camelot, Lanceour spotted Balyn, riding ahead of him. "Balyn!" he shouted. "At last. Prepare to die!"

Balyn pulled on his reins and turned to face Lanceour. "You should not have followed me. You think you frighten me, fool?"

"You killed an innocent woman. Your time has come. Make ready, Knight!"

The two knights jumped down from their horses, drew their swords and circled each other. They fought long and hard, until Balyn saw his chance. With a single stab to the chest, Sir Lanceour fell lifeless to the ground.

It grew dark. A cold wind blew through the trees, but Balyn did not ride on. He stood beside the dead man, lost in his thoughts. He was full of sadness, for Sir Lanceour had been a brave young knight. He did not hear as a maiden rode up to him. When she saw Sir Lanceour lying on the ground, she cried out, rushed to his side and cradled him in her arms.

"Balyn," she sobbed, "You have done a terrible thing. For you have killed one body but two hearts. Two souls are lost today."

Then, trembling, she drew a dagger from her dress. Balyn tried to wrestle it from her, but she turned it on herself and fell across the body of Sir Lanceour, whom she loved more than life.

The moon rose and fell.

When morning came, Balyn had not moved from the spot. His brother Balan, who he loved more than anyone in the world, rode up and found him there. But not even Balan could console him.

"Come, brother. We must leave," Balan said, "I will help you to make amends for this."

"I must defeat King Rience," Balyn said. "If I can, do you think King Arthur could forgive me?"

"I hope so," said Balan. "We can try."

Days later, Balyn and Balan were riding through a dark forest, when a tall, cloaked figure stepped into the road in front of them.

"Who goes there?" asked Balyn.

"I will not tell you my name," said the stranger, whose face was hidden by his hood.

"Then you are an enemy."

"You are Balyn," the man said quietly. "And that is your brother, Balan. You go to meet King Rience. And you will not get very far unless you heed my advice."

"Merlin!" whispered Balan, and he bowed deeply. "We will be ruled by your words."

"Follow me," said Merlin, "and you shall accomplish a brave deed…"

Merlin told them where they could ambush King Rience. They surprised him in the forest, fought fiercely with his men, captured him, and set out with the prisoner to find King Arthur.

They came upon Arthur in the thick of a terrible battle, fighting against twelve rebel kings. All that day, his enemies had held the field and Arthur felt sure that his men would be defeated, until a pair of knights came flying out of the forest.

They rushed into the fray from behind and fought so fiercely that Arthur's foes thought an entire new army had appeared. Soon, the rebel kings had all fled.

"Who were those brave knights?" Arthur asked Merlin, when the battle was over.

"Balyn and Balan, the bravest of men," he replied. "They have brought King Rience to you as a prisoner. But their tale shall be the saddest of any, for they shall both die on the same day."

Arthur had no time to dwell on their sad fate, for he had more battles to fight. Next, he rode north to put Saxon invaders to flight. One day, he saw a knight riding by with a look of terror on his face. A little while later, King Arthur saw Balyn riding past, although he looked so pale and gaunt that at first Arthur hardly recognized him.

"Balyn," he called, "I have reason to be grateful to you. Please, stay awhile."

"Sire, I must not stay. There is a curse upon me, and wherever I go I bring evil," Balyn replied. "But please tell me if there is any way that I can serve my kingdom."

"A man rode past here in some distress. Bring him to me, so I may help him," Arthur said.

"I am at your command," Balyn replied. He bowed deeply and rode off in search of the stranger.

When he reached him, deep in the forest, the stranger turned to him with wild eyes. "Get away from me! Do not stop me — I must flee!" he cried. "There is a black enchantment following me. I must ride on."

There was a whir of wings as a bird took off from the undergrowth and the stranger looked around, startled.

"You have my protection," Balyn assured him. "Come with me. King Arthur has asked for you – he will help you."

"You cannot protect me. No one can!" said the stranger.

"I will protect you with my life," Balyn promised.

So the stranger, who was called Sir Harleus, rode back with Balyn to Arthur.

"King Arthur, this man—" Balyn began, but he stopped short as, out of nowhere, a spear came hurtling through the air and pierced Sir Harleus's chest.

The knight fell from his horse and Balyn rushed to him.

"That was the false knight Garlon," the dying man gasped. "By magic, he rides invisible. It was just as I feared. Please, take my horse. I beg you, avenge my death."

Then, clutching at Balyn's sleeve, he died.

Balyn vowed to take his revenge on Garlon. He sped off straight away, in search of him. On his journey he heard many more stories of innocent people Garlon had slain. But he could not find where he had gone – until finally a stranger told him that Garlon was staying with King Pelles, at the enchanted Castle Carbonek, where a great feast was going to be held the next day.

Balyn galloped through the night. In the

morning, he arrived at the gates of Castle Carbonek, where he was made welcome.

Servants brought him fine clothes and showed him where he could rest before the feast. That evening, as he entered the banqueting hall, a serving man took his sword, for no man was allowed to go inside armed. But Balyn had a small silver dagger clasped in his hand and hidden in the folds of his cloak.

"Which knight is Garlon?" he asked one of the other guests.

"He's over there," the guest replied. "He's the most marvellous man alive," the man chuckled, "he can ride invisible and slay whoever he likes."

"If I kill him here at the feast, with all these knights present," Balyn thought, "I may not escape alive. But if I leave him living, there's no knowing what harm he may do."

"Hey, you there!" Garlon snarled at him. "What are you looking at it? Eat your meat, and get on with what you came here to do."

Balyn walked up to him, slowly and deliberately. "What I came here to do? This is what I came here to do!"

Balyn drew his dagger, and plunged it into Garlon's heart.

The hall exploded into chaos.

"Why have you killed my honoured guest, Garlon?" cried King Pelles. "You shall not leave this castle alive!"

"Kill me if you dare!" Balyn shouted back.

"Garlon was my knight, and I shall avenge him!" roared King Pelles. He grabbed a great

sword from the wall and swiped at Balyn with a
stroke so hard that Balyn's dagger shattered into
a thousand pieces.

Balyn fled, with King Pelles hot on his heels.
He ran along stone corridors and dark passages,
until he came to a flight of winding stairs that
led up into a tower. They were covered in
cobwebs and dust – nobody had set foot there
for hundreds of years.

Balyn raced up the stairs,
stopping at the top to catch
his breath. He found
himself in front of a
closed door and was
suddenly filled with
fear at what could lie
behind it.

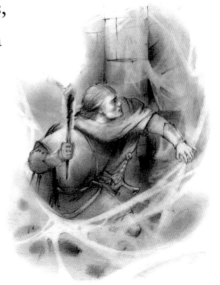

King Pelles' footsteps were crashing up the stairs behind him. Steeling himself, he burst through the door. As he did so, he heard a voice roaring: "ENTER NOT – FOR YOU ARE NOT WORTHY!"

Terrified, Balyn shut his eyes. But when he opened them again, there was no one there.

On the far side of the room there was a table. On the table was a cup covered with a silver cloth. And although the rest of the room was thick with dust, the table and the cloth were shining, and the cup glowed so brightly he could hardly bear to look at it.

Balyn began to tremble. He didn't know why, but he wished to kneel before the table and pray, and never take up a sword again.

He turned to see King Pelles, looming in the doorway. Balyn grabbed at a spear that was hanging on the wall, just as the king dropped his own dagger.

As if by magic, all the rage seemed to fall from the king's face. He stood in the doorway, smiling at Balyn as innocently as a child. But Balyn was taking no chances. He rushed at King Pelles with the spear and struck him in the side.

King Pelles cried out and tumbled backwards down the stairs.

The castle reeled.

Darkness engulfed Balyn. A great wind whirled around him. He was falling through endless darkness...and all he could hear were terrible cries of pain, echoing into the distance.

'Darkness engulfed Balyn. A great wind whirled around him.
He was falling through endless darkness...'

For three days, Balyn lay in the ruins of the castle. It was Merlin who dragged him out, his hair and clothes covered in dust. Merlin held a flask to his lips, and Balyn gulped the water thirstily. "The guests at the feast..." he began.

"All dead. And many others with them," Merlin replied. "Look as far as you can see. What is before you?"

"Ruins," said Balyn. "Wasted lands."

"All because of that one stroke. The spear you used was sacred. The cup you saw was the Holy Grail. Our Lord Jesus drank from it at the Last Supper. King Pelles will suffer from that wound for many years, before he is healed."

Then Merlin helped the feeble Balyn onto his horse.

"Ride on now, Balyn," he said grimly. "Your

destiny is waiting for you, as mine is for me."

So Balyn rode through the wasted lands, past ruined buildings and parched fields. Everywhere he went, people stared at him with empty eyes.

Finally, he came to a castle where he was greeted by a hundred maidens and a hundred knights. The lady of the castle came forward.

"Sir Knight, you are welcome at my castle," she said. "Here you may rest, after all your sorrows."

For the first time in many months, Balyn almost smiled.

"But first you must fight with the Black Knight of the River," the lady said. "All those who enter the castle must pass him."

"I do not wish to fight," said Balyn.

"It is but one battle," the lady said, smiling

gently at him. "Then you may rest."

So Balyn gritted his teeth and rode to the river, where a fearsome stranger was waiting for him. He was dressed in black from head to foot and wore a vizor which covered his face.

In silence, they set their lances. Then they rode so hard at each other that both lances were shattered and each was thrown from his horse.

The two knights lay on the ground for some minutes, before they both struggled to their feet. First, Balyn struck the Black Knight – but the knight struck back with a colossal blow that shattered Balyn's shield. They swiped at each other again and again, until blood flowed from them like water.

At last the Black Knight sank to the ground.

"Tell me your name," Balyn said. "For I never

'First, Balyn struck the Black Knight – but the knight struck back
with a colossal blow that shattered Balyn's shield.'

knew a knight so strong, except my brother."

"My name is Balan," the Black Knight said. "I am brother to the good knight Balyn."

At this, Balyn fainted to the ground. With the last of his strength, Balan crawled over to him. He unlaced his helmet and gently pulled it off. When he saw his brother's face, he wept.

Balyn opened his eyes. Looking up at his brother, tears rolled down his own cheeks. "Brother, what have I done?" Balyn whispered. "I would have known you, if only you had worn your shield..."

Then, clasping each other's hands, the two brothers lay down side by side and died. They were buried beside the castle in the same tomb, and their sad tale was told throughout the land.

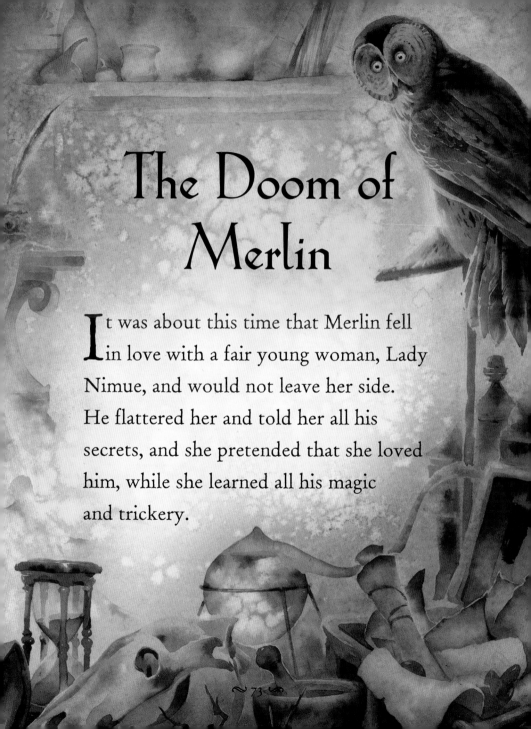

The Doom of Merlin

It was about this time that Merlin fell in love with a fair young woman, Lady Nimue, and would not leave her side. He flattered her and told her all his secrets, and she pretended that she loved him, while she learned all his magic and trickery.

One morning, Arthur was riding alone through the forest, when Merlin stepped onto the path in front of him.

"Let me bid you farewell," said Merlin. "I am leaving Camelot, never to return."

"No! Merlin, you must not. I forbid it!" Arthur replied.

"It is my destiny," said Merlin softly. "Soon, I will be buried alive."

"Impossible! Surely, your arts will save you from any evil enchantment?" Arthur protested.

"My fate awaits me and I cannot escape it," Merlin said simply. "Now, listen to my words, for a time will come when you would rather have my wisdom than all the gold in the world. Take care of Excalibur. Beware the evil woman who shall steal it from you. At the very last, it will be her son who strikes you down."

Merlin looked into the distance, as if he could see the future unravelling there. "She will be with you to the end, although at the last her grasping heart will be washed of all its evil. Now I must go, for Lady Nimue will bury me in the earth, while I still breathe."

Merlin looked gravely at the young king. "One more thing, Arthur, you must remain strong, even when you stand alone."

Then he turned and walked slowly into the forest, and Arthur watched until he was lost from sight.

"Merlin is wise," Arthur thought, "but he is

not right about everything."

Only a year before, Arthur had met a
beautiful maiden called Guinevere. He had fallen
deeply in love with her and wanted to marry her.
But Merlin had warned him against it.
"Guinevere is beautiful and intelligent," he had
said. "And I know that once your heart is set on
its course, nothing will change your mind. But I
beg you, pick another bride."

Arthur had not listened to Merlin then. And
now he and Guinevere were as happy as could
be. Every day, Arthur was more and more
dazzled by his beautiful queen, and the whole
court was charmed by her beauty and kindness.

"No, Merlin is not always right," thought
Arthur, as he rode back to Camelot.

Merlin set out with Lady Nimue and they

travelled through many lands. One day, they were passing a group of boys playing in a field. Merlin stopped and called one of them over to him. "Lancelot?"

The boy nodded.

"When this lady comes for you, ride to King Arthur's court with her," Merlin told him. "There you must ask Arthur to make you a knight. Tell him that it was Merlin's last wish. Now go!"

The boy ran off, with the wizard's strange words ringing in his ears, and Merlin watched him go. Now his last task was complete, he knew what awaited him.

For many days, Merlin travelled with Lady Nimue. He grew to love her more and more. But she was soon bored. She had learned all of his

magic and now she longed to
be rid of him.

One afternoon, they came
to a great hawthorn tree,
bursting with bright white
flowers.

There, Nimue sat against the trunk of the
tree, and Merlin rested his head in her lap and
shut his eyes. The journey had wearied him.

Then Nimue gently rose and began to sing,
weaving a spell around him with her voice.

Merlin slept, and in his dreams he was inside
a magic tower. It was the strongest tower in the
world. When he awoke, he could not move.

"Lady, you have drawn all my magic from
me," Merlin said. "Do not leave me here alone,
with these strange dreams. Stay with me a little,"

he pleaded. But Nimue only shook her head.

Then, as if he was in a trance, Merlin got to his feet. He walked down a narrow stairway which had appeared in the ground before him. Down and down he went, under the earth.

In pitch blackness, he felt his way along the tunnel until he came to a large room, and he lay down on a great slab of stone and shut his eyes.

He could still hear the faint, sweet sound of Nimue singing. As it grew fainter still, he knew there was no way back towards the light.

Nimue soon went on her way. Time passed and grass grew over the spot, so no one could ever find it.

For all that is known, Merlin lies there still. There he shall stay, until the day he awakes, when Arthur's kingdom shall be restored.

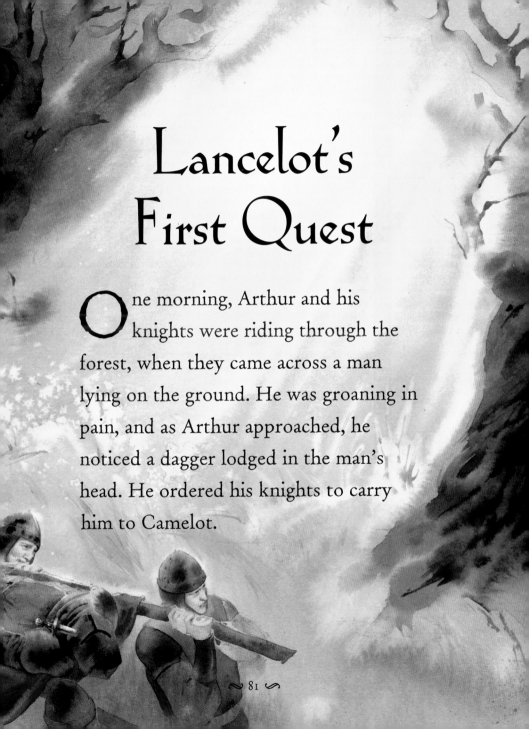

Lancelot's First Quest

O ne morning, Arthur and his knights were riding through the forest, when they came across a man lying on the ground. He was groaning in pain, and as Arthur approached, he noticed a dagger lodged in the man's head. He ordered his knights to carry him to Camelot.

The knights laid the wounded man down in the Great Hall, and he beckoned Arthur to his side. "Now I am at your court, I shall be healed," he whispered. "Here I shall find the best knight in the kingdom. His first great deed will be to draw out the dagger and heal my wound. The enchantress Lady Nimue told me that this would be so."

It so happened that all of Arthur's knights were gathering at Camelot that day. Arthur and Guinevere were holding a feast, for it was a year since their wedding, and Arthur had invited his knights to celebrate with them.

He looked on with pride as the knights took their places at the Round Table in the centre of the hall. Every knight had an equal place at the table, so no man could complain that he was set at the lowest end. The table had been a gift from Merlin, and it was full of a powerful magic. When a new knight arrived at Camelot to serve Arthur, his name would appear in gold on one of the seats at the table, and when a knight died, his name would quickly fade away.

Most mysterious of all was the Perilous Seat. Merlin had told Arthur that this seat was destined for Arthur's most valiant knight. If anyone else dared to sit in it, they would die instantly. No one had yet dared try.

When all of Arthur's knights were seated, Guinevere entered the hall, dressed in her finest silks. Arthur smiled as he gazed at her. "No man on Earth is as happy as I am today," he thought, as he rose to his feet. "Knights of the Round Table," he declared, "it is lucky that you are all

here to celebrate with me, today. One of you –
my finest knight – will be able to heal this
wounded man by pulling out the blade. Before
we eat, go to his aid, for he suffers greatly."

One by one, Arthur's knights tried to pull
out the dagger. But none of them succeeded, not
even Arthur's nephew Sir Gawain, who was his
favourite knight.

"Do not despair," Arthur told the wounded
man. "Perhaps a marvel awaits us today."

No sooner had he said these words than the
door opened and Lady Nimue appeared, with
three young men beside her. The first of them
was so handsome that when Guinevere looked
at him all the colour fled from her face.

"My name is Lancelot," the young man said.
"Merlin's last wish was that I should come here

and ask you to make me a knight."

"See how his name grows in gold upon the empty seat…" said Lady Nimue.

Arthur watched as the name appeared in glowing letters upon the empty seat at the Round Table. He beckoned Lancelot, and the young man knelt before him. Then Arthur took Excalibur and laid it upon one shoulder and then the other. "Arise, Sir Lancelot," he said.

Next, he turned to Hector and Lionel and knighted them too. Then Lady Nimue took Lancelot's hand and led him to the wounded man. Very gently, Lancelot reached over and drew out the dagger. The wound closed before their eyes, and the man got to his feet as though he had never been hurt. He thanked Lancelot, and took his leave.

Lancelot and his cousins joined the other knights at the Round Table and the feast began. But some of the older knights were disgruntled by Lancelot's easy entrance to the Round Table. "Look at that innocent face," one muttered. "How can he be a knight so young? He's practically a child!" another joined in.

Listening to the knights' chatter, Lancelot said nothing. But silently he vowed to become the best knight that he could possibly be.

As the knights ate and drank and danced, Lancelot looked in wonder at the hall around him and at the king and queen in all their finery. He could not help staring at Guinevere, for he had never seen any woman so graceful. But when she looked up and smiled at him, Lancelot's whole body turned cold and he felt almost as if he had been struck.

In that moment he knew as clearly as he knew that grass was green, or the sky was blue, that he would never love any woman but Guinevere. Privately he took a solemn vow to devote himself to serving her, faithfully, as a knight.

Early the next morning, Lancelot woke his cousin Lionel. "Get up! Today we will ride out on our first quest. We shall not return to Camelot until we have had a great many adventures!"

They strapped on their armour and rode into the forest in the early morning light. The sun grew hot and at noon they rested under an apple tree. Lancelot fell into a deep sleep, while Lionel kept watch. Before long, he saw three knights in the distance, streaking across the meadow on horseback. A huge, strong knight came after them. As Lionel watched, the biggest knight overtook the others. He struck each one, felling them from their horses. Then he dismounted, flung the knights over their saddles, took up their reins and led them away.

"Here I may win great honour," Lionel thought to himself. So he sprang onto his horse, and chased after the knight, riding as hard as he could. Very soon, he caught up with him.

"Turn! Defend yourself! Or release those men you attacked!" Lionel yelled.

The knight turned, set his lance, and raced towards Sir Lionel. He struck him so hard that Lionel was thrown from his horse. Then he tied Lionel's hands and feet, threw him over his horse and led him away with the others.

At Camelot, Hector was looking for Lancelot and Lionel. Thinking that they must have set out in search of adventure, he rode off into the forest to find them. Hector rode for a long time, until he came across an old man.

"Tell me," he said, "do you know of any place nearby where knights seeking adventure might have gone?"

"A mile from here is a tall castle by a river. A famous knight named Sir Tarquin lives there. Beside the river there's an oak tree, and hanging on the tree are many shields. They belong to knights that Sir Tarquin has overthrown and cast into his dungeon. Strike the copper basin beside the castle and Sir Tarquin comes out to fight."

Hector thanked the old man and rode on, and soon he found himself staring up at the oak tree.

Its branches were encrusted with shields... including the shield of Sir Lionel.

In fury, Hector struck the basin. A moment later, a huge knight came riding out of the castle, a lance in his hand. "Come, joust with me!" the knight boomed.

Hector charged, and his lance struck Sir Tarquin's shield so hard that both man and horse spun around.

"That was well done!" Sir Tarquin shouted. "You hit me as a brave knight should. That makes my heart leap for joy!"

Then he rushed at Hector, lifted him clean out of his saddle on the point of his lance, carried him into the castle and threw him onto the cold stone floor. Hector squinted up at Sir Tarquin's grinning face.

"You are a mighty jouster," said Tarquin, chuckling. "So I'll spare your life." Then he picked up Hector with one hand and threw him into a hot, filthy dungeon.

There were more than one hundred knights in the dungeon. Hector searched the sea of wretched faces and at last he saw that of his dear brother.

"Lionel! What happened?" he cried.

And so Lionel told him the whole story. "And I left Lancelot," he concluded, "sleeping under an apple tree…"

Lancelot was still there, sleeping peacefully under the apple tree, when four queens rode past. One of them was Arthur's half-sister, the enchantress Morgan Le Fay, who practised dark magic. As soon as Morgan saw his handsome face, she wanted him to be her love. So did each of her companions.

"Let's not quarrel over the fair knight," said Morgan Le Fay. "I shall cast a spell on him. He shall sleep for seven hours, and when he awakes, he will be in my castle. Then he can choose one of us to be his mistress."

When Lancelot awoke, he saw that he was in a stone cell, and a young maiden was laying out bread and water for him. "The knight awakes," she said, giving him a shy smile.

"Unhappily, yes," said Lancelot gloomily. "Where am I? This must be some foul enchantment."

"I will return and tell you more," she said quickly. "I cannot speak now." She rushed from the room, locking the door behind her.

The next morning, Lancelot was dragged before the four queens, seated on four thrones.

"Welcome, Lancelot," said Morgan Le Fay. "You look surprised, but of course I know who you are. Merlin foretold that one day you would be the finest knight alive. I see in your heart that you love Guinevere alone. Yet now you shall lose her, or else lose your life. For you shall never leave this castle until you choose one of us to be your lady and your love."

"A difficult choice," Lancelot replied. "To die, or to choose one of you to be my love."

Morgan smiled. She knew that of all the queens, she was by far the most beautiful.

Lancelot looked her in the eye and said, "I'd rather die than shame my honour. You are all wicked, false enchanters!"

"You refuse us?" said Morgan, unable to believe her ears. "You choose death?"

"By my life," shouted Lancelot, "I refuse the whole, poisonous lot of you."

When he said these words, the four queens all started screaming at once. They threatened Lancelot with terrible tortures, and Morgan Le Fay's soldiers dragged him back to his cell.

As Lancelot lay there, wondering what cruel

fate Morgan Le Fay would dream up for him, he heard soft, swift footsteps. The door opened a crack. "Lancelot?"

The maiden had returned with food and wine. "How are you faring?" she asked.

"Not too well," he replied.

The maiden shut the door behind her. "Perhaps I can help you," she whispered. "I do not care for Morgan Le Fay—"

"Help me," Lancelot begged, "and I will repay you in any way that is honourable."

"In that case," she answered, "do battle for my father at the tournament next Tuesday."

"I shall," Lancelot promised.

"Tomorrow morning, listen for my knock and be ready. I shall lead you to your escape," said the maiden.

All night, Lancelot lay awake. In the early morning, he watched a bar of light as it crept across the ceiling. He waited, and waited – until at last he heard a tap at the door. It opened, and the maiden beckoned him. They tiptoed through the corridors, until she unlocked the last door and led Lancelot to the field outside, where his horse was waiting for him.

The maiden told him where to find the tournament. Then she watched as he galloped away into the mist.

The next week, Lancelot rode to the tournament on behalf of the maiden's father. Dressed all in white so no one could recognize him, he stormed onto the field, and easily overthrew all his opponents. Then, without waiting for thanks, he rode away in search of

'Dressed all in white so no one could recognize him, he stormed onto the field, and easily overthrew all his opponents.'

another adventure.

Soon enough, Lancelot rode into a clearing where Gaheris, Gawain's younger brother, was jousting against an enormous knight. As Lancelot watched, Gaheris tumbled to the ground and the knight picked him up, threw him over his saddle, picked up the reins and galloped away.

Lancelot raced after him, yelling, "Turn, Sir Knight! Defend yourself!"

The knight stopped, turned and glared at Lancelot. "Are you are a Knight of the Round Table too?"

Lancelot nodded.

"Excellent! I defy you, and all your fellowship!" the knight boomed.

"That's enough talking," said Lancelot. "Let us fight."

So the men lowered their lances. They rode apart, then turned and rushed at each other. Each knight hit the other's shield so hard that their horses reared and fell, throwing both men from their backs. The men stumbled to their feet and fought on the ground, hammering blow after blow with their swords.

"You are the mightiest knight I have ever met!" said the enormous knight. "It would be a shame to kill you. But as I am the enemy of King Arthur and all your fellowship, I will not rest until one of us is dead!"

With that, he ran at Lancelot. They

fought bitterly, until Sir Lancelot saw his chance and, finally, sliced off his opponent's head.

Gaheris, who had awoken and was watching, spoke up. "How can I ever thank you?" he said. "You saved my life. And not just my life. By killing Sir Tarquin, you have saved the lives of many other knights…" Then Gaheris told Lancelot all about Sir Tarquin's castle and the many knights trapped in his dungeon.

The fight had left Lancelot with deep wounds. But he ignored the pain as they set off together through the forest to find Sir Tarquin's castle.

By nightfall, Lancelot and Gaheris had arrived. While Lancelot went to wash his wounds in a stream, Gaheris flung open the dungeon door. "Arise, knights!" Gaheris shouted. "You are free!"

For a moment Hector, Lionel and all the other knights were speechless. Then they greeted Gaheris like a hero, but he silenced them. "Lancelot is the one you should thank," he explained. "He vanquished Sir Tarquin, whom no other knight could defeat."

Hector and Lionel stumbled out of the dungeon to find Lancelot and thank him. But Lancelot had already ridden away.

On and on he rode for many weeks, through forests, mountains and wild places. He rescued many maidens, vanquished many evil knights, and felled giants and dragons with his lance.

By the time Lancelot returned to Camelot, his fame had spread throughout the kingdom. For in swordfighting or jousting or any sort of battle, no man had ever beaten him.

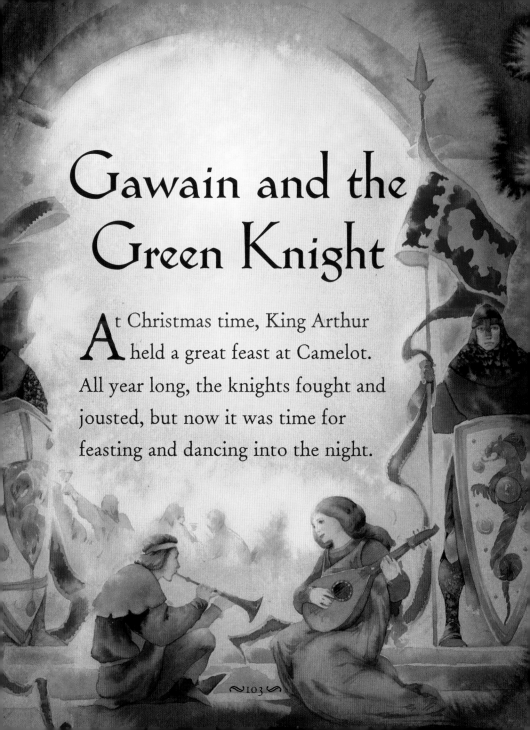

Gawain and the Green Knight

At Christmas time, King Arthur held a great feast at Camelot. All year long, the knights fought and jousted, but now it was time for feasting and dancing into the night.

The celebrations lasted for a full fifteen days, and on New Year's Eve King Arthur sat with Guinevere, brimming with happiness, as the knights took their places at dinner. Arthur was watching and waiting, for he had pledged that he would not eat until he had seen a marvel or heard a stirring tale of men at arms.

Then, just as a fanfare of trumpets piped in the first course, the door burst open and a stranger filled the doorway.

He could almost have been a giant. He was a mountain of a man with a fine, handsome face. But what made everyone gasp was that he was entirely emerald green.

His skin was green. His hair, which tumbled to his waist, was green. He was seated on a horse that was green from its ears to its hooves. His tunic and cloak gleamed with green jewels. Only his eyes flashed red.

In one hand the stranger held a sprig of holly and in the other an enormous, glinting axe. He entered the hall on horseback, cantered the full length of it and stopped in front of Arthur. "Are you in charge of this rabble?" he roared.

The knights stared, speechless, but Arthur merely said: "A warm welcome, sir, on this winter's night. My name is Arthur and I rule this house. Won't you join our feast?"

"I've no time to waste," said the stranger. "Your men are known as the finest knights in the world. If they really are so brave, I'd like them to join me in a simple game."

"Are you here to fight?" Arthur asked.

The stranger laughed. "Fight? Your puny

lightweights wouldn't last a second against me!
If I wanted a fight, I wouldn't have left my
sword and spear at home. No, I simply ask
whether any man here is brave enough to strike
me with this axe and receive one blow in return.
I'll kneel and take the first blow. After that, they
have a year and a day to seek me out and receive
my blow. So, will anyone take me on?"

He held up the glinting weapon and scanned
the sea of stunned faces before him, but no one
answered.

"So, this is the famous Camelot!" he snorted.
"Look at you all trembling in your seats. I
haven't even lifted a finger!"

He laughed so loudly that Arthur sprang up
from his seat. "Your request is foolhardy," he
said, "but if you really want someone to chop off

your head, I'll do it."

So the stranger handed Arthur the heavy weapon and calmly knelt and bowed his head. But as Arthur heaved the axe into the air, his nephew Gawain stepped forward.

"Wait!" said Gawain. "If you allow me, I will take your place in this trial. Such a foolish game is not fit for a king."

Then the other knights joined in, all of them backing Gawain. So Arthur nodded and Gawain came forward, taking the weapon in his hands.

"Take care to cut him cleanly," Arthur whispered.

"Well, Gawain," said the stranger, "you understand the rules?"

"I must strike one blow," said Gawain. "Then I'll have a year and a day to seek you out, and receive a blow in return."

The Green Knight nodded, swept the hair from his neck and bowed his head again, without a flicker of fear.

Gawain lifted the axe high in the air – and struck. The Green Knight's head rolled across the floor and blood soaked his green robes.

Gawain stepped back, relieved that his grim task was done. But the body didn't slump forward or fall sideways to the floor. Instead it stood up, stomped across the hall, grabbed its head by its ropey hair and mounted the horse.

"Sir Gawain, you can find me at the

Green Chapel," the Green Knight's head said. "Come by on New Year's morning, one year from now, and you'll get what you deserve. Come, unless you want to be called a coward forever."

With that, he spurred his horse into a gallop, and was gone.

The feast began and soon enough the hall rang with laughter. But all the while Gawain stared into space, stroking the back of his neck.

Seasons passed. As summer gave way to autumn, Gawain decided it was time to set out on his unhappy quest. King Arthur solemnly wished him well, and knights and ladies wept as he rode away from Camelot upon his horse, dressed in his finest golden armour. Nobody expected to see him again.

For months, Gawain searched through many wild lands for the Knight of the Green Chapel. He rode through dark, tangled forests and up steep mountain slopes. He trekked for lonely days along sea cliffs. He fought bears and boars, dragons and giants, and went on enough adventures to fill a book of tall tales. And wherever Gawain went, he asked: "Have you heard of the Knight of the Green Chapel?"

But no one had ever heard that name.

On Christmas Eve, he found himself in a forest of dark trees, their leafless branches lined with snow. Chilled to the bone and hungry, he mumbled a prayer that he would find a chapel, so he could go to mass on Christmas Day.

No sooner had he spoken the words, than he saw the spires of a castle rising above distant trees. "Thank God," he muttered, "a refuge."

When he rode up to it, he found a castle more impressive than any he had ever seen. A watchman welcomed him through the gates, and in the grand hall, a handsome man strode up to him, beaming. "Welcome," he said warmly. "I am the lord of this house. Please, treat my house as your own."

Then servants eased off Gawain's armour and brought him fine clothes to wear. Soon he was warming his feet by a fire, with a thick fur cape around his shoulders.

That night at dinner with his host and his host's beautiful wife, Gawain ate well, drank deeply, and felt life seeping back into his bones.

"So, tell me a little about your life," his host said, when Gawain had eaten his fill.

"I come from Camelot. My name is Sir Gawain," he replied.

The lord burst out laughing. "Gawain, your bravery is famous throughout the land. You are more than welcome in this house. My only request is that you do not ask my name."

So Gawain spent three days feasting and making merry with the lord and his wife. On the third day, he made ready to set out.

"Gawain, why are you leaving us so soon?" his host asked.

"I have a quest," Gawain replied. "I must find the Knight of the Green Chapel by New Year's Eve. In three short days I have to face my destiny, and I would rather die than shirk my duty."

The lord laughed. "Relax! The Green Chapel

is not more than two miles away. Stay with us, and on New Year's Day I will send a guide to show you the way. Save your farewells for then."

"In that case," said Gawain, "let me serve you in any way I can while I stay with you."

"Do you mean that?" his host asked.

Gawain nodded.

"In that case, I have a game for you," said his host, with a grin. "Tomorrow I will be out hunting all day. My wife will keep you company while I'm gone. But let's make a pact. Whatever I win in the woods will belong to you, whatever you win while I'm away will be mine."

"Why not?" said Gawain. "Let's drink to it."

So, the next day, the lord rose before dawn and set off to hunt. The air was soon thick with arrows as the hounds and horses flew through the forest, racing after a herd of deer.

Meanwhile, Gawain dozed in bed. Half asleep, he heard a sound, and looked through a gap in his bed curtains to see the lady of the house creeping into his room. Gawain shut his eyes. He pretended to be asleep as he heard her pull back the curtains and sit down softly on the edge of the bed.

He lay there for some time, wondering what had brought on this strange visit and hoping that she would leave. When she didn't, he stretched and opened his eyes.

"Good morning, Sir Gawain," the lady said. "You slept so well that anyone might have wandered in here. And now," she giggled, "you are trapped!"

"Good morning," said Sir Gawain, sitting up in bed. "I will do whatever you ask of me, but first, let me dress. Then we can talk more easily."

"Nonsense," the lady replied. "I'd much prefer to stay just as we are. My husband is out, the servants are snoring, my maids are away and the door to this room is barred with a bolt. I have an honoured guest, a brave knight, and I will take my time to talk to him."

"You flatter me," Sir Gawain replied uncomfortably, "I'm sure I don't deserve such rich praise."

"Good knight, nothing would give me greater pleasure than talking to you. I'd rather be here with you than have all the gold in the world."

"You are too kind," said Sir Gawain.

They talked for hours of many things and finally the lady got up to leave. At the door, she turned back to him.

"You are noble, handsome and polite. But you are not the famous Sir Gawain."

"Why not?" Gawain asked.

"Sir Gawain would never be so rude as to let a lady leave without a kiss."

"Very well," said Sir Gawain. "If a kiss is all you ask for, I shall keep my promise."

He kissed her, and she returned his kiss and left without another word.

That night the host returned from the hunt and showed Gawain his haul – a huge pile of venison. "Well, what do you think?" he asked.

"It's a fine result," Gawain replied.

"It's all yours, according to our bargain," said his host.

"And whatever I've won between these walls belongs to you," said Gawain. So he gave him a kiss, just as the lady had given him.

"Now Gawain, your gift would mean more to me, if you told me where you had won it," said the host, a smile playing on his lips.

"That wasn't the agreement, so I shall not answer," Gawain replied.

That night they shared a feast by the fire and agreed to play again the next day.

Early the next morning, the lord and his men leaped from their beds to join the hunt. The hounds raced through thickets and forests, until they sniffed the scent of a wild boar.

It burst out of a thicket, hurtling past the

men and trampling the hounds. The lord tore after the beast, chasing him until dusk, when finally, in a river, man and beast faced each other.

As they clashed, the lord slashed the boar's neck and burst his heart.

Gawain was still snoring when the hunters set out. But the lady had not forgotten him. She crept into his room again and sat down on his bed. "If this is Gawain who greets me, then I am disappointed that he has neglected the first rule of honourable behaviour," she said.

"Which rule?" asked Gawain sleepily.

"You should have kissed me, of course," said the lady. And so Sir Gawain gave her a kiss, which she returned. Again, they talked for hours.

"How can it be that you, an honourable knight, have not talked to me of love?" the lady

'Gawain was still snoring when the hunters set out.
But the lady had not forgotten him.'

asked. "All the tales of famous knights tell how knights live for love and lay down their lives for love. And yet of love you have not spoken to me a single word."

"In faith, I know little of love," Sir Gawain replied, blushing. He changed the subject and they talked some more. All the while, she gave him smiles and loving looks, which Gawain politely ignored. In the end, she asked for a kiss. He kissed her once more and she left.

That night, Gawain's host gave him the enormous boar, and Gawain gave him the two kisses he had won that morning. After dinner, they sang song after song, and the lady and Gawain sat together all the while. And so loving was the lady to Gawain, sending him smiles and inviting looks that he felt half mad with desire.

And the lord and Gawain agreed to play the game a third time the next day.

At dawn, the hunting horns rang through the woods and the huntsmen rode through the forest, after a fox. They chased him for miles, while the wily fox kept running ahead, with the baying hounds hard on his heels.

Gawain lay in bed that morning, dreaming of the Green Knight. In his dreams he heard the knight sharpening his axe, and saw the steel blade crashing down towards him. He woke with a start, to find the lady sitting on the end of his bed, frowning at him.

"How can you sleep on this beautiful morning?" she asked. "Wake up, Gawain. Let us talk." So they talked for some time and then the lady grew serious and quiet. "Gawain," she said, "will you not give me some gift that I might keep as a memory of you?"

"My lady," Gawain said, "you deserve the highest prize that I could offer. But all I have is a glove. It would be far too lowly a gift for you."

"Well then, do not give me a gift. Still, here is mine for you," she said, and offered him a ruby ring from her finger.

"I cannot take this," Gawain said, "since I have no gift to give you in return."

"Then take this belt," she urged him, unbuckling a beautiful green belt from around her waist.

"By God's grace, I cannot take this either. I must refuse,

no matter how flattered I am," he said.
"I give you thanks, a thousand times over."

"If you knew its powers, you would not
refuse it," the lady said. "Whoever wears this
belt will be safe from his enemies. He could face
all the cunning and strength of a thousand giants
and never be slain."

Gawain looked again at the belt in her hands.
With luck, it could save his life. As she pressed
him to take it, he gave in. The lady begged him
not to mention a word of this to her husband,
and he agreed, thanking her with all his heart.

For his thanks, he was repaid with three
kisses. When the lady had left, Gawain dressed
and hid the belt beneath his clothes.

That night, the lord came into the hall,
holding a fox, and Gawain gave him three kisses.

"I'm sorry that all I have for you is this puny fox," said the host. "It's not much compared to your three kisses."

"Enough," said Gawain. "We have completed our pact." But he said nothing of the magical belt he had won.

That night the feast was merrier than ever before, and it was with a heavy heart that Gawain set out the next morning.

A wild wind whipped across the land and sleet battered the ground as Sir Gawain rode away from the castle. Hidden beneath his armour, he wore the silken green belt.

An old servant led the way until they came to the edge of a forest. "Gawain, you are close to the chapel that you seek," the old man said. "But the place you are going is perilous indeed. There lives a wild man who loves murder more than he loves his own life. If you find him, he will kill you. Take another road, Sire. I swear, I won't tell a soul."

"Thank you," Gawain said. "Your words are kindly meant. But I must be true to my vow."

So Gawain rode on into the forest and soon he came to a bleak-looking valley, with cliffs on both sides that reached up into the sky like jagged teeth. The Green Chapel was nowhere to be seen. Instead, ahead of him was an old cave, covered with moss. As Gawain walked up to it, he heard a sound that made his blood run cold. It was the sound of metal being scraped across stone.

"Are you there?" Gawain shouted to the echoing cliffs. "I've come to honour my pact.

You had better be quick – it's now or never."

"Wait," came a voice from beyond the cliffs. "You'll soon get what I promised you."

Eventually the grinding stopped and a moment later the Green Knight came charging out of a dark hole in the cliffs, with the axe held high above his head.

He leaped down to where Gawain was standing. "Welcome, Gawain, after all your wandering," he roared. "You know the vow made between us. Last year I took your blow. Now I have one to give you in return. So take off your helmet and kneel before me. Show no more fear than I did when I gladly lowered my head and you severed it with one blow."

"I will not hesitate," Gawain replied, though all the colour had drained from his face. He knelt down and the knight lifted the axe. With all his strength, he aimed a savage blow.

If the axe had met Gawain's neck, he would surely have been a dead man. But Gawain shrank back, and the axe hacked through the snow and bit into the ground beneath.

"Call yourself brave?" the Green Knight snarled. "Call yourself honourable? I didn't so much as *blink* when you struck me. I've never met such a cowardly knight."

"I flinched at first, but I will not fail," Sir Gawain said defiantly. "Try me again. I will not move, I swear. Deal me my destiny."

Then Gawain knelt and shut his eyes, knowing his life had reached its end.

"Take this!" the knight roared as he raised the axe and sliced down through the air. But the axe stopped dead, hovering just an inch above Gawain's bare neck. Under the axe, Gawain was as still as a stone.

"Now you've shown a bit of courage, I'll despatch you properly," the Green Knight said.

"Then get hacking," growled Gawain. "Your threats mean nothing to me."

"By God, I'll slice off your head right now!" The Green Knight heaved the axe high in the air and let it drop but, at the last moment, he veered away and Gawain was left with just a nick in the side of his neck. A splash of bright red blood stained the snow.

Gawain leaped to his feet, grabbed his spear, thrust on his helmet and turned to face his enemy. "You've had your swing now!" he shouted. "I've taken one blow without hitting

'Gawain knelt and shut his eyes, knowing his life had reached its end.'

back. Try me again and I'll attack you."

The Green Knight stepped back and looked Gawain up and down. He saw how light he was on his feet, how proudly he held his sword.

"Be a little less bold, young man," he said calmly. "I've done nothing more than what we agreed in the Court of King Arthur. I promised you one strike, and I've dealt it. If I'd wanted to slice off your head with a single blow, I could have. My first blow missed you. That was only fair, in keeping with the contract we made that first night, when you promised to give up all you won to me."

At these words, Gawain felt as if he might faint to the ground.

"Then I missed you again, for the following day you kissed my wife and then kissed me.

Twice you told me the truth, and twice I left you unscathed. The third time you strayed, and so you felt my blade."

Now Gawain's face was burning with shame.

"The belt you wear beneath your armour is mine," the knight said. "It was woven by my wife and so I know it well. I sent her to test your loyalty and found you to be the most faultless fellow on earth. Your only fault was that you loved your life."

Sir Gawain stood there for what seemed like an eternity. Then he took the belt from around his waist and flung it to the ground. "A curse on greed and fear! They breed villainy and destroy virtue!" he shouted. "I was afraid of the axe. My fear made me forget the loyalty which every knight knows. Tell me, how can I clear the name

I have shamed?"

"Your confession is enough," the Green Knight replied. "I declare you are as innocent as the day you were born. Please, take the belt and wear it to remember our meeting. Now, come with me to my castle, where a feast awaits us!"

"Thank you," said Gawain, "I've stayed here long enough. But I will wear this belt, as a sign of my weakness." He jumped up onto his horse. "One more thing before you go, good sir, what is your name?"

"My name is Bertilak de Hautdesert," the Green Knight said. "It was my guest, Morgan Le Fay, who dreamed up this plan. I believe she expected you to stray — and lose your life."

So Gawain bade the knight goodbye and rode away, and he went on many more adventures before he came back to Camelot.

Upon his return, Gawain told his tale before the whole court, still ashamed of his weakness. "But Gawain," King Arthur protested, "this story shows your strength as much as your weakness."

"Still, I will wear the green belt for evermore, to remind me of what happened," Gawain said.

The other knights of the Round Table promised that they too would wear green belts under their armour as a sign of their union with Gawain. His strength was their strength, and his weakness their weakness.

The Wickedness of Morgan Le Fay

One afternoon, Arthur and his knights were out hunting. Hot on the heels of a hart, they chased it to the shores of a lake, where the hounds caught up with it. As Arthur sounded his horn to end the hunt, a ship came gliding across the still waters of the lake.

Its sails were white and the air that filled them was heavy with the scent of violets. When Arthur stepped aboard, he found that the ship was empty.

"Come, let us explore this strange ship," he said to his men. Sir Accolon, one of his knights, and Urien, Morgan Le Fay's husband, followed him on board. They explored the ship and found cabins hung with rich, rare silks and beautiful tapestries. When they climbed back on deck, night had fallen, and the deck was lit up with hundreds of glowing torches. They watched in astonishment as the shore began to slide away from them. The ship was sailing by itself across the smooth lake.

Then twelve maidens silently appeared on deck, offering the men the finest meats and wine.

As they ate, strange melodies filled the air. After dinner, a maiden led each man to his own richly furnished cabin and, before long, the three men were deeply asleep.

The next morning, Urien opened his eyes to find himself back in Camelot. He had no idea how he had got there. His wife, Morgan Le Fay, was lying in bed beside him, with a dangerous light dancing in her eyes.

When Arthur awoke, he found himself in a dark dungeon. The air was filled with terrible groans. "Who are you that call out in the darkness?" he asked.

"We are twenty knights, all prisoners," a feeble voice replied.

"How were you trapped?"

"The lord of this castle is a man called Sir

Damas," the voice said. "He took this castle from his brother, Sir Outlake. All those who pass by, he takes prisoner."

As soon as he said these words, the dungeon door swung open and a maiden shone a lamp into the darkness.

"How are you faring?" she asked Arthur.

"Not so well," he replied.

"Sire, you can win your freedom if you will fight for Sir Damas. Today his brother is sending a champion to fight, and whoever wins the battle will be lord of this castle and these lands."

"Sir Damas is an evil knight," said Arthur. "I would not choose to defend him. But I would rather fight than die in this dungeon. If Sir Damas agrees to free these knights, then I will fight for him."

"It shall be so," the maiden said. She led Arthur out of the dungeon and gave him a horse and some armour. All the other knights were freed, while Arthur prepared to fight.

At the same time, Sir Accolon opened his eyes, and found himself staring up into a cloudless sky. He was lying on the very edge of a deep well. As he turned his head, he saw that if he had rolled just an inch to the left, he would have fallen to his death.

He jumped to his feet. "I was tricked!" he thought. "Those women were fiends! If I ever find them, I will slay them and all those who practise evil enchantments!"

Just then, a dwarf approached him. "I come from your lady, Morgan Le Fay," the dwarf said. "She sends all her love."

Sir Accolon smiled. Morgan Le Fay was his mistress, and he was devoted to her.

"She begs you to fight today with an unknown knight for her sake," the dwarf continued. "For this task she sends you King Arthur's sword Excalibur and its scabbard. When you fight, you must show no mercy."

The dwarf held out the sword in his hands, and Sir Accolon recognized the jewelled hilt.

"Have no fear," said the dwarf, "victory will be yours. Morgan's husband, Urien, is about to die, killed by a traitor. Morgan bids me to tell you that when he dies, you may wed her. Then Arthur will be defeated, and you will rule together."

Sir Accolon took the magic sword and felt the thrill of its strength as he held it. With Excalibur in his hands, he would surely be victorious. "I suppose the enchanted ship was all her doing too?" he asked in wonder, and the dwarf nodded.

For many months, Morgan had hinted to Sir Accolon about her schemes, telling him to be ready when the time came. "Now, I will prove my love," Sir Accolon thought. "Now it begins."

So the dwarf led Sir Accolon to the castle of Sir Outlake, and left him in a fair green meadow, where squires gave him armour.

Far over the other side of the field, King Arthur was strapping on the armour he had been given, when a maiden greeted him. "I come from your sister, Morgan Le Fay," she said. "I bring your sword, Excalibur, which you left in her keeping. Here is the sword and the scabbard. My mistress prays for your safety."

King Arthur thanked the maiden. Now he had Excalibur, he would fight with a light heart, for its scabbard was enchanted, and he who wore it would never lose any blood, however deeply he was wounded. So he put on his helmet and strode out onto the field to face his opponent.

Just like Arthur, Sir Accolon was wearing plain armour and a closed vizor, so neither man recognized the other. First they fought with lances, and when those were broken to bits, they drew their swords and sprang at each other like lions. But as Arthur fought, his sword felt brittle and weak. With every stroke, Accolon's sword cut through his armour and soon Arthur felt blood pouring from his wounds. But when

Arthur's own strokes hit home, his opponent did not spill a drop of blood. Soon, Arthur was sure that some evil magic had been used to switch the swords and that the true Excalibur was in his opponent's hand.

"Beware, knight – this battle is mine!" Accolon roared, as he struck Arthur with an almighty blow. Arthur staggered backwards and then ran at his enemy, using the last of his strength to strike at his enemy's helmet. Sir Accolon fell to the ground but Arthur's sword shattered to pieces.

"You must surrender!" said Accolon, staggering to his feet. "You have no weapon! Surrender at once or I will slice off your head!"

"I vowed to fight to the death," said Arthur through gritted teeth. "Though I lack a weapon,

I will not lack honour. If you kill me here, unarmed, it is you who will be shamed."

"Run or be slain!" roared Accolon, and he slashed at Arthur again. But Arthur held up his shield and rammed Accolon so hard with it that he dropped his sword.

Arthur snatched it up. At once, power surged into his arm, and his heart leaped, for he knew it was Excalibur. "You have been away from me far too long," he whispered. "Look what damage you have done!"

Arthur darted forward, snatched the enchanted scabbard from his enemy's side and hurled it as far as he could away from them.

"Sir, you have done great damage with my sword today," said Arthur. "But now it is time for my sword to repay you. Prepare to face your death."

With that, Arthur struck the knight so furiously that he fell to the ground, his helmet breaking into a thousand pieces.

"Now I will slay you!" Arthur thundered.

"I have never seen a knight fight so bravely," gasped Sir Accolon. "But I have vowed to fight to the end. Kill me if you will."

Arthur paused for a moment, catching his breath. Though the man was filthy and covered in blood, he thought he recognized him. "What is your name?" he asked.

"I am Accolon, from King Arthur's court," the man replied.

A wild fury swept through Arthur. "Then how did you come by this sword?" he asked with a trembling voice.

"Morgan Le Fay gave it to me," Accolon told him. "I have loved her for a long time. I vowed that I would fight whoever she asked me to, even if it was Arthur himself. She told me that if I fought this battle, I would rule with her. But that is all over now. I am ready to die. But tell me, who might you be?"

The king took off his helmet. "I am Arthur," he said.

Accolon gasped and began to weep. "Sire, forgive me! Have mercy on me," he whispered.

"You came here plotting my death. You are a traitor," Arthur said. "But you shall have mercy, Accolon. It is Morgan Le Fay's sorcery that brought you to this, so it is she who must be punished. She has betrayed me – her brother and her king. My vengeance will be known throughout the kingdom."

He helped Accolon to his feet. "We are both gravely wounded and must rest."

So Arthur went and made peace between the two brothers, Sir Outlake and Sir Damas. And as dusk fell, Sir Outlake led Accolon and Arthur to an abbey nearby, where monks tended to their wounds. Sir Outlake stayed beside them, praying for their recovery. Arthur soon gathered his strength, but Accolon was too badly wounded. Four days later, he died.

With a sorrowful heart, Arthur sent for six of his knights. "Take this body to Morgan Le Fay. Tell her it is my gift to her," Arthur said bitterly. "And tell her that I have recovered my sword and scabbard."

In Camelot, Morgan Le Fay believed that her plan had worked. She silently rejoiced that Arthur was dead. Finally, she had defeated him. Now she would kill her husband, Urien, and she and Accolon would rule together. And as she chanced upon Urien sound asleep in bed, she saw her chance.

"Quick! Fetch my lord's sword," she whispered to one of her servants. "Urien will not wake from his sleep."

"Madam," the girl replied in shock. "You cannot kill your husband!"

"Hush girl," said Morgan, "do as I say."

The servant girl ran downstairs to Morgan's son, Sir Uwain, and told him what she knew.

"Be gone," said Sir Uwain. "I will stop her, but she must not know you have spoken to me."

The girl nodded silently and, with trembling hands, brought the sword to Morgan Le Fay.

Then Morgan tiptoed to the bed where her husband lay sleeping. She drew back the curtain and looked at him for a moment. "Poor Urien," she thought as she raised the sword...

But Sir Uwain rushed into the room and seized her arm.

"What are you doing?" he shouted.

He wrenched the sword from her hands. "You are a fiend, a devil! If you were not my mother, I would slice off your head this very moment!"

"Forgive me," said Morgan, crumpling to the floor. "I was led astray. Do not denounce me, I beg you! I vow, from now on, I shall never be tempted to any kind of violence again."

"Keep your oath and I will not betray you," Sir Uwain said.

"I swear it with all my heart," said Morgan.

That night, Morgan was brooding on a new way to kill Urien, when one of her handmaidens brought her the news that Accolon was dead, and that Arthur was resting at an abbey in the forest.

Morgan knew that she had to think quickly. Soon Arthur would be coming for her. Within the hour, she was riding away from Camelot with forty of her knights by her side. She rode night and day, afraid for her life.

But instead of riding away from Arthur, she rode to the abbey where he was recovering. If she acted quickly, she thought, she might be able to steal Excalibur before he used it against her. "May I visit Arthur?" she asked the abbess at the gate.

"He is sleeping," replied the abbess.

"I am his sister," Morgan replied. "It would cheer me greatly to pray by his side."

So the abbess led her to a small, plain room,

where Arthur lay asleep with Excalibur clasped in his hands. The enchanted scabbard was on the bed beside him.

"My poor, dear brother," Morgan murmured. Turning to the abbess, she said softly, "Please leave me alone with him while I pray."

The moment the abbess was gone, Morgan snatched the scabbard and fled.

When Arthur awoke, he saw at once that the scabbard was missing. "Who was here while I slept?" he asked.

"Only your sister," the abbess said.

"You have failed me!" Arthur burst out. "I said that no one was to be admitted! Bring me a horse and fetch Sir Outlake at once!"

So the wounded Arthur mounted his horse and he and Sir Outlake rode through the night, on the trail of Morgan Le Fay. By dawn they had been joined by more of Arthur's knights. Arthur asked a cowherd if he had seen anyone riding by.

"Yes, Sire. A lady, Sire, with forty men. She rode that way." The cowherd pointed ahead, and so they raced on.

Finally, as dusk fell, they caught sight of Morgan and her knights. "Halt!" Arthur called.

But Morgan raced into the forest. She came to a lake and hurled the scabbard into the water. Then she led her knights off into the trees.

Suddenly she found herself in an empty, stony valley, with high cliffs on all sides. She reined her horse to a halt as her knights galloped into the valley behind her. Morgan's eyes scanned the sheer walls of the valley in panic. Arthur would be upon them any moment.

'She raised her arms and, in an instant, she and her knights were
transformed into standing stones.'

They were trapped.

Shutting her eyes, Morgan began to murmur an enchantment. She raised her arms and, in an instant, she and her knights were transformed into standing stones.

Seconds later, Arthur and Sir Outlake broke through the trees. They stared around at the silent valley. "Strange. I could have sworn they came this way," said Arthur. But there was no one in sight, so they turned and rode away.

Night fell, and slowly the stones began to move as the knights came out of their enchantment. Rubbing their cold limbs, they followed Morgan out of the valley.

Morgan rode on, further and further away from her brother. She had escaped. But from that day on, she lived in fear of Arthur's revenge.

The Adventures of Lancelot

O f all the knights at Camelot, the greatest was Lancelot. He was always ready to battle evil knights, sorcerers, giants and dragons. No other knight had his strength or his skill, his kindness or his courage...

But Lancelot was not the perfect knight. From the first moment he had set eyes on Guinevere, he had loved her. At first, he had vowed to serve her faithfully as a knight. But as the years went by, Lancelot's love for Guinevere grew stronger and stronger. When he could no longer bear to see her, or dance with her, or listen to her sweet voice without wanting to steal her away from his king, Lancelot rode away from Camelot to try to forget her.

One day, he was riding through a strange, barren land, when he came to a hilltop village, overlooked by a dark tower. As he approached the village, an old man called out: "Lancelot – thank God! A lady is trapped in the tower and only you can save her."

"I will try," Lancelot replied.

So the old man led Lancelot to the tower. Once inside, they walked up a spiral staircase, until they came to a heavy iron door.

"Behind this door is the fair Lady Elaine," the old man whispered. "Morgan Le Fay was jealous of her beauty, so she used dark magic to trap her here. No man has been able to set her free. But I know that you will."

On the inside, the door was covered in heavy iron bars, but as Lancelot rushed at it, the bars shattered and he burst through to find Elaine chained to the wall. As Lancelot took her by the hand, the spell broke. The chains melted away and she fainted into his arms, unharmed.

Lancelot carried her gently down the stairs and as they came out onto the street, she stirred in his arms and awoke. "My rescuer," she said.

"How can I ever thank you for saving me?" She smiled up at him and Lancelot saw that she was just as fair as the old man had said. "Good knight, will you take me home?" she asked.

"Most gladly," said Lancelot, helping her to her feet.

"Before you go, good knight," the old man said. "A beast has laid waste to our town..."

Lancelot did not hesitate for a moment. "Where may I find it?" he asked.

The old man pointed to a stony outcrop beyond the village and Lancelot set off at once. As he got closer, he saw a cave. He crept up to it, hoping to surprise whatever lay inside. But as he reached it, the beast rushed out. It was a dragon: monstrously huge and breathing fire. It rushed at him and, with one quick swipe of its claws, broke

'It was a dragon: monstrously huge and breathing fire.'

his shield in two. As Lancelot stumbled backwards, it roared, sending an enormous ball of fire shooting towards him.

Lancelot's armour was burning hot, but he threw himself at the dragon – stabbing and slicing, though his sword kept glancing off the dragon's tough hide. They fought for hours.

Then, just as the dragon coiled its body ready to pounce, Lancelot darted forward and, with one colossal stroke of the sword, he sliced off the beast's head. The dragon crashed to the ground.

Lancelot's wounds burned like fire, but he rode back to Elaine to accompany her home as he had promised. Her home was the haunted Castle Carbonek. Elaine was the daughter of the famous King Pelles, who had been wounded long ago and whose wound had never healed.

Lancelot had heard strange stories of Castle Carbonek and the desolate lands around it. As they rode towards the castle, they passed ruined buildings, dried-out rivers and people with hunger in their eyes. Inwardly, Lancelot shuddered, for it seemed as if there was a curse on the land.

But when they arrived, all the ladies and knights of the castle rushed to greet them with cries of joy. Lancelot put all dark thoughts from his mind as he sat down to a lavish supper with his host, the wounded King Pelles.

"My everlasting thanks for bringing my daughter back," King Pelles said. "Please, stay with us a little while."

So, for many days, Lancelot stayed at Castle Carbonek, while Elaine tended to his wounds.

She spent every day by his side and soon she had fallen deeply in love with him. But Lancelot's love for Guinevere burned stronger than ever and he barely noticed her.

After some weeks, Elaine asked an old enchantress who lived in the castle whether there was any way she could win Lancelot's heart.

"Lancelot loves only Guinevere," the old woman said. "But do not weep. I know a spell which will win his love for a little while. Then you will have a child, who shall be called Galahad. He shall cure your father's wound, and restore these cursed lands. And he shall be the best knight that the world has ever seen."

So, that night, Elaine slipped away from the castle in secret. A little later, a messenger arrived for Lancelot and told him that Guinevere was staying at a castle nearby. At once, Lancelot galloped out into the night. When he arrived at the castle, Guinevere welcomed him inside with smiles and kisses. Soon Lancelot forgot all about his loyalty to Arthur.

The next morning, Lancelot lay in bed beside his love. But when he opened his eyes, he saw that it was not Guinevere but Elaine lying beside him. He sprang out of bed.

"Forgive me!" said Elaine, bursting into tears. "I enchanted you because I love you—"

Lancelot did not wait to hear any more. Overcome with grief and shame, he fled from the castle, out towards the hills.

For many months, Lancelot wandered in the wilds, without knowing where he was. In the spring, when he had still not returned to

Camelot, his cousin, Sir Bors, set out to find him. On his way, he came to Castle Carbonek, where he met King Pelles and Elaine, who was holding a newborn child in her arms.

"This is my son, Galahad. Lancelot is his father," she said, smiling proudly. "One day, he shall be the greatest knight in the world."

Then she told Sir Bors of Lancelot's visit and how he had run away into the hills. Sir Bors searched and searched for Lancelot, until finally

he found him sitting under a tree, looking as weary as an old man.

He led Lancelot to a hermitage, where he nursed him back to health. It took many months but when

Lancelot was finally well enough, they returned to Camelot together.

There, everyone was delighted to see Lancelot – except Guinevere, who greeted him coldly. "Why did you leave for so long?" she asked as they strolled through a garden together. "Did some fair lady win your heart?"

"There is only one person I love," said Lancelot quietly. Then, trembling as he spoke, Lancelot confessed his love to the queen. When he had finished speaking, they said no more words to each other. But after that, they no longer tried to keep apart.

And though Lancelot was still the bravest of Arthur's knights, his love for Guinevere hung like an iron chain around his heart.

Sir Gareth

One day, when Arthur's knights were all gathered at Camelot, a young man was escorted into the hall by two burly knights. "This ruffian will not tell us his name and yet he wants to speak with you," one of the knights said. "I will hear him," said Arthur.

"Most noble king," the young man said, "I ask you to grant me three gifts. I promise they shall not be unreasonable, nor cause you harm."

Arthur liked the young man's fair and honest appearance and he answered, "Ask what you will, and you shall have it."

"I request food and drink for one year," the young man said. "When that time has passed, I shall make my other two requests."

"Don't ask for something so small!" Arthur replied. "Anything you ask for shall be yours."

"Meat and drink is all I ask for," the young man said quietly.

"In that case, you shall have it. But first, tell me your name," Arthur said.

But the stranger shook his head. So Arthur called for his brother, Sir Kay, and asked him to look after their mysterious visitor.

"Treat him as if he were a lord's son," he told Sir Kay. "He may turn out to be one of our bravest fighters one day."

Kay snorted with laughter. "If he were a warrior, he'd want a sword and armour, not pies and ale!"

Sir Kay called to the stranger. "Follow me, and I'll show you to your quarters. Tell me, what's your name?"

"I cannot say," the young man said, as Kay led him towards the kitchens.

"Rumour has it, you'd rather eat than fight," Kay went on. "I suppose it's because of those delicate hands of yours. I expect you don't want to ruin them by picking up a sword. In fact, I've got a perfect name for you – Sir Lovely Hands!"

He pointed to a small, dirty corner in the kitchen. "That's where you'll sleep, Sir Lovely Hands," he said. Then he walked away, chuckling to himself.

For a year, the stranger worked in the kitchens. He scrubbed the floors, prepared the meals and did everything that Sir Kay asked, without ever complaining. Sir Kay delighted in calling him 'Sir Lovely Hands', and working him until his hands were raw.

Whenever he wasn't working, the young man watched the other knights as they jousted and fought – especially Lancelot. He studied Lancelot's every move.

A year later, King Arthur was at dinner with his knights, when a young woman rushed into the Great Hall and stood before Arthur.

"My name is Lady Linnet," she said. "I beg you to help my sister, Lady Lionesse. She is trapped in her castle by a fearsome tyrant. It is my hope that one of your brave knights may defeat him."

As she said these words, Sir Lovely Hands stepped forward. "King Arthur, I thank you for the hospitality you have shown me this past year. And now I ask my two other gifts of you. Firstly, that you allow this quest to be mine. Secondly, that Lancelot shall ride with me until I am worthy to be made a knight, for I wish to be made a knight by Lancelot alone."

Arthur looked at the young man, dressed in

his kitchen boy's tunic. He had never seen him hold a sword. But determination and bravery shone in his pale blue eyes.

"I grant your request," he said, and Lady Linnet's face turned to thunder.

"I ask for your help," she said, "and you send me a skivvy from your kitchen? When you have Sir Lancelot and Sir Gawain – the best knights in the world – seated before me?"

In a fury, Lady Linnet stormed out of the hall, mounted her horse and rode away from Camelot. Moments later, Sir Lovely Hands was galloping after her. When he caught up with her, she turned on him. "You! You come here, stinking of kitchen grease, and presume to help me? Get back to your pots and pans!"

"I vowed to King Arthur that I would help

you," he replied. "So I will help you, or die in the attempt."

At this, Lady Linnet burst out laughing. "Is that right? Out in these woods, you'll meet a real fighter before long. Then you'll wish you were in your kitchen, scrubbing saucepans."

"We'll soon see," he replied.

So they rode along together, in silence.

Before long, a knight dressed all in black appeared on the path before them.

"The Knight of the Black Lands!" Lady Linnet gasped. "Run away, boy, before he cuts you to shreds!"

"I'm no coward," Sir Lovely Hands said, as the Black Knight called out, "Fair lady, is this your champion?'

"No, indeed he is not," said Lady Linnet.

"He's a mere kitchen boy. He's nothing to me."

"In that case," said the Black Knight, "I could do with his horse. Come kitchen boy – let's see you fight!"

"With pleasure," said Sir Lovely Hands.

They lowered their lances and charged at each other like bulls. As they clashed together, Sir Lovely Hands' lance pierced the Black Knight's armour and he fell from his horse, stone dead.

Lady Linnet turned to him. "You are a coward. You slew him by treachery!" And she cantered off into the distance.

But Lady Linnet wasn't the only one watching the fight. Lancelot had followed Sir Lovely Hands as he rode through the forest. And when Sir Lovely Hands bent to put on the Black Knight's armour, he stepped forward.

"That was a valiant fight," he said. "I will gladly make you a knight, if first you tell me your name."

Sir Lovely Hands fell to his knees. "My name is Gareth," he said quietly. "I am the younger brother of Gawain and Gaheris. But they do not know me — they have not seen me for ten years."

"Go forth, Sir Gareth," said Lancelot joyfully. "Fight with great courage. There will be a place for you at the Round Table when you return."

Lancelot turned to ride back to Camelot and Sir Gareth set off once more after Lady Linnet.

When he caught up with her, she shouted, "Away, boy! I'm

really not fond of the smell of kitchen grease. The fighters in these woods will soon make mincemeat of you."

No sooner had she spoken than a knight dressed in green came riding towards them. "Tell me, is that my brother, the Black Knight, riding with you?" he called, recognizing his brother's black armour.

"No," said Lady Linnet. "It is a kitchen boy who murdered your brother."

"He died in a fair fight!" Sir Gareth cried.

But the Green Knight was already charging at him. As their lances clashed, they broke in two. The two fighters jumped to the ground, drew their swords and flew at each other. Before long, Sir Gareth was standing over the Green Knight.

"Let me live!" the Green Knight pleaded. "I

will serve you, and so will my thirty knights."

"I will gladly spare you if Lady Linnet allows it. Lady Linnet, what is your will?"

"You – a kitchen boy – have thirty knights at your service? I don't think so."

"Then he must die," said Sir Gareth, lifting his sword into the air.

"Wait!" said Lady Linnet. "He is a fine knight. Spare his life. "

So the Green Knight was spared and he vowed to serve his mysterious opponent, even though Sir Gareth would not reveal his name.

The next day, as they rode on through the forest, a knight dressed in blue appeared. "Are you my brother, the Black Knight?" he called.

"No, he is the knave who murdered the Black Knight and beat your other brother the Green

Knight by trickery," said Lady Linnet. "Take your revenge!"

Without another word, the Blue Knight went flying towards Sir Gareth. They fought for more than two hours, with Lady Linnet watching.

"Blue Knight," she said. "Must it take so long to beat a mere kitchen boy?"

At these words, the Blue Knight threw himself at Sir Gareth, but Sir Gareth ducked and as the Blue Knight tumbled to the ground, Sir Gareth wrenched off his helmet. He stood over him, ready to slice his head from his shoulders.

"Let me live, and I will serve you," the Blue Knight blurted out.

"If the lady permits it," said Sir Gareth.

Lady Linnet frowned. "He can hardly be worth killing if he couldn't defeat you," she said.

And so they rode on again. But still Lady Linnet continued to abuse Sir Gareth. "You must turn back now, you fool! Soon we will reach my sister's castle, guarded by the Knight of the Red Lands. Only a knight as strong as Lancelot or Gawain could beat him. Now, run away – coward that you are!"

"Lady Linnet, you insult me. You deny the brave deeds I have done. But I have not run away yet and I do not intend to run away now. I will not break my promise to help your sister."

His speech was so courteous and polite, Lady Linnet was taken aback. "You really mean to fight the Knight of the Red Lands, knowing he has never been beaten?"

"Of course," said Sir Gareth.

"You will surely lose your life!"

"I am not a coward," Sir Gareth said again.

At this, Lady Linnet's proud face crumpled. "I am sorry," she began. "I never believed that a kitchen boy could be so brave. I see now that you are a fearless fighter. How stupid I have been! But why should you help me, when I have been so cruel to you, despite your deeds?"

"When your cruelty made me angry, I turned that anger against my opponents," Sir Gareth said calmly. "Now your kindness gives me joy. I will use that joy to bring me victory."

"But...who are you?" Lady Linnet asked.

"My name is Sir Gareth," he replied, "brother of Sir Gawain. At Camelot I told no one who I was. I wanted to know who my true friends were. I wanted to prove myself by my deeds, not by my noble family."

"Can you ever forgive me?" she asked.

"It is already forgotten," he replied.

They rode on and, within a few hours, they reached the castle of Lady Lionesse. Beside it was a terrible sight – a tree, with more than forty dead knights dangling from it.

"What can this mean?" whispered Sir Gareth.

"This is the work of the Knight of the Red Lands," said Lady Linnet. "All these knights tried to rescue my sister."

"And where may I find the Red Knight?" said Sir Gareth, without a flicker of fear on his face.

"If any man wishes to fight the Red Knight, he must blow the horn hanging in the tree and the Red Knight will come," said Lady Linnet. "But do not blow it yet! He has magical powers. Until noon he has the strength of seven men."

"Then either I will beat him honourably, or die today," said Sir Gareth, riding up to the tree. He took the horn from the branch and blew it so loudly that it was heard for miles around. As the sound echoed through the valley, a young maiden appeared at a castle window.

"Look up," whispered Lady Linnet, "and you will see my sister, Lady Lionesse."

Sir Gareth looked up and there, gazing down at him, was a beautiful young woman. She smiled sadly at him. "I will fight gladly for her," he said, "and she will be my lady."

"Then you have not a moment to lose," said Lady Linnet. For the Knight of the Red Lands was already riding out of the castle gate, looking as strong as a boar.

"Don't stare at my lady like that," he bellowed. "What you are looking at is mine!"

"You trapped her," Sir Gareth replied. "You know that she doesn't love you. Who could love such a man?"

The Red Knight snorted.

"Know too that I will rescue her, or die in the attempt," Sir Gareth said.

"Think of the knights you have already seen this morning," said the Red Knight. "Do you really want to join them?"

"You think that sight will frighten me? It only gives me more courage to defeat you."

"Enough talk," the Red Knight said. "Prepare to die!"

The Red Knight slammed down his vizor, and they both set their lances and charged. They collided with such force that both were knocked to the ground.

For a moment both men lay on the grass, unable to move, before they staggered to their feet, reached for their swords and hurled themselves at each other.

They fought in a whirl – hacking, jabbing, striking at each other. They fought until blood poured from their bodies, until they hardly knew where they were – and they picked up each other's swords in the confusion.

All the while, Lady Linnet stood watching and Lady Lionesse looked down from the window, praying for her champion.

As the sun set, they were still exchanging blows. When they were both bleeding so badly that they could barely stand, they rested on the ground for a moment. Glancing upwards, Sir Gareth saw Lady Lionesse smiling down at him from her window. She gave him such a sweet, tender look that he was full of fire.

"Come! Let us fight to the end," he said. And with an almighty roar he threw himself against the Red Knight, who dropped to the ground, his sword spinning out of his hand. Sir Gareth's sword was at his chest.

"Spare my life," the Red Knight begged.

"You have never shown mercy to anyone. And yet I will spare you, if Lady Lionesse will allow it. Will you spare him, Lady Lionesse?" Sir

Gareth called up to her.

From her window, Lady Lionesse nodded. Then the castle doors were opened and Sir Gareth rushed inside to find Lady Lionesse. He knelt before her, and humbly asked her to marry him. "I accept with all my heart," she said.

The couple spent a very happy winter at the castle. When spring came, Gareth set off for Camelot to take part in a tournament. Just before he left, Lady Lionesse gave him a ring. "Wear this, my love, and no one will know you," she said. "Today you may prove yourself as a knight before the whole court."

So Sir Gareth slipped the ring onto his finger and galloped off to the field to fight. All day, as he jousted and fought, the colours of his armour shimmered, changing constantly. One moment he was in yellow, the next in red, then green, then black.

As Arthur watched, he was astonished by the mysterious knight. At the end of the day, he declared him the champion. "I have never seen a fighter like you," Arthur said. "Please tell us your name."

Sir Gareth slipped the ring from his finger. "I am Sir Gareth, brother of Gawain and Gaheris," he said. "I have returned to serve you."

Arthur was overjoyed, as were Gawain and Gaheris, who rushed forwards to embrace their brother. That night a banquet was held and Sir Gareth took his place at the Round Table. When he looked across at his brothers and at Lancelot, he thought he might burst with pride.

Sir Gawain and Lady Ragnell

E arly one morning, Arthur was hunting in the woods, when a white hart appeared in a clearing before him. As the beast darted off through the thicket, Arthur whispered to his men, "Stay here. I will follow him on foot."

Taking his bow, Arthur crept after the deer until it stopped for a moment to graze on some grass. Arthur took aim and let his arrow fly, and the deer tumbled into the thicket.

As Arthur ran forward to take his catch, a colossal knight stepped into his path and struck him to the ground.

"Well met, Arthur!" cried the knight, drawing his sword. As he pointed it at Arthur's chest, Arthur felt his body turn as cold as ice.

"Gromer Somer Joure is my name," the knight boomed. "And your life, King Arthur, is in my hands."

Arthur tried to leap up

to fight, but he found that he could not move a muscle. His arms and his legs were frozen, as if held by some black enchantment.

"You must do my bidding, or lose your head," the knight said grimly. "With the magic that I wield, I could kill you now. But I shall give you one chance to save your life."

"It seems I must accept," Arthur replied.

"Good. Then follow this quest. Discover the one thing that women most desire. Return to me here with an answer in a year from now, and you shall go free. But if your answer is false, I will slice your head from your shoulders and present it to my mistress, Morgan Le Fay. Now, go!"

The knight leaped up onto his horse and galloped off through the trees, his laughter echoing through the forest.

Slowly, warmth crept back into Arthur's limbs. He blew his hunting horn, and when his men rushed to his side they found Arthur sitting next to a dead hart with a sorrowful look on his face.

That night, Arthur told Gawain of his strange quest. "All I know is that I must find the answer or lose my life," he said sadly.

"You must," said Gawain. "But you shall not do it alone."

And so, for a year, while most of the other knights set out on their own quests, or fought in battles, Gawain and Arthur travelled through many lands, asking every woman they met the answer to the riddle.

Some women answered friendship, some said laughter, youth, admiration, or love. Arthur and

Gawain wrote down each answer in a large, leatherbound book, and rode on.

When the year had passed, they returned to the forest to meet Gromer Somer Joure. But Arthur was full of dread, because he felt in his heart that he had not yet found the right answer. As he rode, he thought of Merlin, and wished that he was with him now, for he feared that his death was close at hand and he did not know who else could help him.

Their journey was nearly at an end when they came across a lady mounted on a fine, white horse. She was dressed in rich velvet robes and wore exquisite jewels. But when Arthur looked at her, he shrank back, for she was the ugliest woman he had ever seen.

Her face was blotched red and wrinkled like a

prune. Her eyes were tiny and peered out from under a heavy, knitted brow. Her teeth were yellow and curved like boar's tusks over her lips. And she was as round as a barrel with old, wrinkled hands that looked like lizard's claws.

"Greetings, King Arthur!" the old woman said. Arthur was so shocked by her strange appearance that for a moment he did not reply.

"You should not lose your tongue, Arthur," she said, "for I know well why you are riding through this wood. And today your life depends on me."

"Forgive me," Arthur replied. "If you can

help me, I shall be forever grateful to you."

"I know of the riddle you must answer this day or die," the lady told him. "And let me tell you, the answers you have found are not worth a fly! But I will tell you the true answer and save your life, upon one condition."

"Tell me and I will grant it," Arthur said.

"That is a rash promise," the lady said. "Do you really mean it?"

"What do you ask?"

"Your solemn vow that one of your fair knights will be my husband."

"That I cannot promise," Arthur said.

The lady's face fell, and Arthur saw a flash of pain and grief in her eyes.

"Then you ride to your death," she replied. She turned her horse to ride away, but Gawain blurted out, "I will take you as a wife, if you will give Arthur the answer. Would you have me as your husband?"

The lady turned back and looked at Gawain. "Do you jest?" she asked, in a gentle voice that did not suit her hideous appearance. "I would not have you laugh at me."

"I do not," Gawain replied.

"Think of the shame I would bring you," the lady said. "You would really marry someone so old and ugly and misshapen as me?"

As he nodded, she started to weep. "Truly, Gawain, you have done a noble thing," she said, before riding up to Arthur and whispering the secret in his ear.

"Now ride on to find Gromer Somer Joure," she said. "My name is Lady Ragnell. Gawain, I shall ride to Camelot, ready to be your bride."

So, that afternoon, Arthur rode to the clearing where Gromer Somer Joure was waiting for him.

"Greetings, King Arthur!" cried the burly knight. "You are brave indeed to meet me here. Now, let's see if you have the answer to my riddle. What is it that women desire most in all the world?"

"I have travelled all over the kingdom," said Arthur. "I bring you many answers, and I am sure that one of them is true."

"Then please, let me hear them," the knight replied, with a cruel smile playing on his lips.

So Arthur opened his book and began to read. "Fine food, laughter, love, kindness, desire..." And he went on, until he had read out every answer he had been told on his travels.

"Ha!" barked the knight. "Arthur, you are a dead man! Your answers are all false. Bow your head, so that I can slice it from your shoulders."

Then, grinning, he drew his sword.

"Stop," said Arthur. "I have one more answer. On my way here I met a loathly lady. She told me that women love many things. They love to be young and beautiful. They love to be flattered. But what they desire above all is power – the power to choose their own destiny."

Then the knight's face fell. "Go!" he roared. "You are free. Go! I shall cause you no harm."

So Arthur rode away through the forest, thankful for his life. At the edge of the woods, Gawain was waiting for him, beaming. "You're free!" Gawain cried.

"I have been freed, but now your punishment

begins. How can I ever thank you? You have saved my life by making your own a misery."

"You saved my life in battle countless times," Gawain replied. "If I had not helped you when you needed me most, then I would be a most terrible coward."

That night, when Arthur and Gawain returned to Camelot, a messenger told them that Lady Ragnell was already there. Gawain would be married the very next day.

So, the next morning, Gawain went to church and found Lady Ragnell waiting to marry him. She was dressed in the finest jewels and embroidered golden robes, which only made her look all the more monstrous.

"I wish that I was less foul, since you are so fair," she whispered to Gawain, as the ceremony

'...she slurped at her wine and tore at the chicken with her teeth.'

began. And then, before Arthur and Guinevere and many knights of the Round Table, Gawain vowed to be true to her for all his life.

After the wedding, a great banquet was held in honour of Gawain and his bride. But instead of congratulating the couple, everyone stared at Lady Ragnell in horror.

They continued to stare as she slurped at her wine and tore at the chicken with her teeth. No one could bear to sit with her, apart from Gawain, who sat silently looking down at his own plate. Not a single knight congratulated Gawain on his marriage.

That night, Gawain went to his bedroom, where he knew his bride was already in bed waiting for him.

"I hope you will not be rude," she said in a

soft, low voice, as she heard the door creak open. "Though I am foul, I am still your wife. So you could at least kiss me."

"Of course I will," said Gawain. Then he pulled back the bed curtains to reveal the most beautiful woman he had ever seen.

"Who are you?" he gasped. "And what have you done with my wife?"

The woman smiled. "I am your wife," she said.

"I don't understand," murmured Gawain. "Today, you were old and misshapen, and now you are fairer than anyone I have ever seen."

He looked at her long red hair, her milk-white skin, and her emerald-green eyes, which looked at him with such kindness and love.

"Are you not happy with your bride?" she asked, and he nodded, amazed.

"Gawain, my beauty will not stay," she said. "There is a terrible curse upon me. You have before you a simple choice and you must choose what is best for your honour. 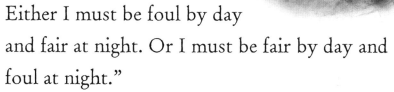 Either I must be foul by day and fair at night. Or I must be fair by day and foul at night."

"There is no other way?" asked Gawain, and the Lady Ragnell sadly shook her head.

"You must decide. If I am foul in the day, the whole court will laugh at both of us. Or, if I am beautiful in the day and admired by the court, I shall be hideous at night while I lie by your side.

Now, make your choice."

"But the pain is yours to bear," Gawain said softly. "The decision must be yours. I put it in your hands."

She looked at him and tears sprang into her eyes, and she fell into his arms, laughing. "Gawain, your kindness has set me free! Now the curse is broken forever. It could only be broken if you gave me the power to choose my destiny. Now I may be fair both night and day. So please, Gawain, kiss your wife."

The next morning, when Gawain walked into the hall with Lady Ragnell by his side, everyone fell silent, dazzled by the beautiful stranger.

"King Arthur," Gawain announced, "this is my wife, Lady Ragnell, who saved your life."

Before the whole court, Lady Ragnell told

Arthur the story of the enchantment. "Gawain rescued me," she said finally. "Because of his great kindness, I swear, I will never anger him in his life."

And it was true. Gawain and Lady Ragnell found true happiness together. And Gawain became an even better knight than he had been before, through his love of her. But Lady Ragnell lived for only five years. And for the rest of his life, Gawain would grieve for her.

Sir Galahad and the Grail Quest

It was the day of a great feast at Camelot. King Arthur and his knights were about to start eating when a young squire rushed into the hall. He was so excited that he forgot his manners and blurted out, "Come quickly! A stone is floating near the river's bank, with a sword lodged in its middle!"

An excited murmur went around the table.

"Let's go and see this marvel for ourselves," Arthur declared. "To the river!"

As the knights and ladies picked their way down to the muddy river bank, Arthur was quiet and thoughtful. The last sword in a stone that he had come across had made him king. What might this one do?

Soon, the stone was in sight. Sure enough, a sword was jammed into it, blade first. Below the sword, letters were etched into the stone:

ONLY MY TRUE OWNER SHALL PULL ME OUT. HE SHALL BE THE BEST KNIGHT IN THE WORLD.

Arthur turned to Lancelot. "That must mean

you," he said.

But Lancelot shook his head. "It can't be me," he replied. He glanced beyond Arthur to where Guinevere stood on the bank. "While I love Guinevere," he thought, "I can never be a good man, never mind the best knight."

Arthur gave him a searching look. "Very well. Gawain, will you pull the sword out?"

Gawain also shook his head. "If Lancelot is not worthy, then who am I to claim I'm a better knight than he is?"

"Come now Gawain. Will you refuse your king?" Arthur laughed. "Try, at least."

So Gawain clambered down to the water's edge and put his foot on the stone to steady it. Then he heaved at the sword's hilt with all his strength. It didn't move an inch.

Next, a brave young knight called Sir Percival stepped forward. "I will try," he said, and he gripped the sword. But tug as hard as he might, the sword stayed stuck.

Arthur sighed. "Perhaps another knight may have better luck another day. But for now, let us go in to dinner."

As they sat around the Round Table, each knight in his accustomed seat, one place lay empty, as always – the Perilous Seat. It was destined for the best knight in the world and anyone else who sat in it would die instantly.

Lancelot took his place on one side of the seat and Percival sat on the other side. Then, just as they raised their goblets to toast the king, the Perilous Seat began to glow.

A great wind battered the castle and all the

doors slammed shut. Then Lancelot gasped as glowing golden letters appeared on the seat:

A KNIGHT WILL COME ONE DAY WHO IS DESTINED FOR THIS CHAIR AND FOR THE GREATEST DEEDS THAT ANY KNIGHT WILL EVER DO.

...which then dissolved into a single line of writing:

HE IS COMING. NOW.

The hall was silent, and every knight had his eyes on the Perilous Seat. Then quiet, slow footsteps echoed through the hush. An ancient man with a long white beard hobbled into the hall. With him was a slender young man in red armour, with no sword or shield, but an empty scabbard hanging at his side. His face shone with a light that seemed unearthly in its purity.

"He looks like an angel," thought Sir Lancelot. But there was another resemblance that struck him to his core. As Lancelot looked into the boy's cool grey eyes, he knew right away that he was his own flesh and blood.

The old man spoke up. "I am Naciens the hermit, of Carbonek," he said. "The boy is Galahad. His mother, Elaine, gave him to me to raise him. I have trained him to fight as well as any knight. He has come to take his place at the Round Table."

Arthur looked thoughtful. He looked from the boy to Lancelot. "I think he does belong here. But I assume that he is not yet a knight?"

"No," said the hermit. "But it is his destiny." He pointed a skinny arm towards the Perilous Seat and everyone watched as glowing letters appeared on it:

THIS IS THE SEAT OF SIR GALAHAD,
THE WORLD'S BEST KNIGHT.

Gazing in wonder at the boy, Arthur nodded. "Lancelot. Knight this boy. For he will surely be the greatest of us all."

Galahad went down on one knee and Lancelot pulled his sword from his scabbard. Touching the boy gently on each shoulder, he said: "Arise,

Sir Galahad."

Sir Galahad stood. "Thank you," he said, then walked calmly to the Perilous Seat and sat down.

Arthur and his knights were wonderstruck. Sir Galahad was sitting on a chair that would be deadly to anyone else. Lancelot's eyes shone with pride. Arthur raised his cup. "To Sir Galahad!"

"To Sir Galahad!" all the knights replied.

After dinner, Arthur took Sir Galahad down to the riverside and pointed out the sword lodged in the stone. "Will you try to pull it out? I should warn you, some of my very best knights have tried and failed. So there is no shame if you can't do it."

Sir Galahad nodded, strode forward, and pulled the sword out of its stony sheath as easily as if he was plucking a flower.

"You are a mighty knight indeed!" Arthur exclaimed.

Sir Galahad shook his head. "It is no great feat. This sword belongs to me, so it responds to my touch. Look, I have an empty scabbard waiting for it."

He slipped the sword into the scabbard at his side. It was a perfect fit. "Naciens told me that this was the sword that Balyn used to slay the Lady of the Lake, and his brother Balyn," Galahad said. "Merlin set it in stone to keep it safe until I was ready."

Arthur shook his head in wonder. "Perhaps you will be able to undo some of the pain that Balyn caused," he said.

The next day, Arthur held a jousting competition in Sir Galahad's honour, and the quiet boy-knight felled every knight who charged him, even Sir Gawain and Sir Gareth.

As they sat down to dinner that evening, the excited talk of jousting was silenced by a roll of thunder. But then the thunder hushed itself and a ray of sunlight fell through a window. It was a far brighter light than any of the knights had seen before.

Everyone around the table seemed to glow with the light, and each man looked fairer to the others than they had ever been before. They all sat in silence, unable to say a word, as a shining cup began to float across the hall, covered with a white cloth. It glowed with such a bright light that no one could look straight at it.

"It is the Holy Grail," murmured Arthur. His

voice was barely a whisper but, in the silence of the hall, everyone could hear him. "The holy cup that caught Jesus's blood as he hung on the cross. The cup that heals all wounds."

Then the floating Grail in its shining cloth faded and was gone. All the knights were silent, filled with a great peace. All except a knight who had not been long at Camelot – Sir Mordred, Morgan Le Fay's son. Arthur saw that he had hidden his face in his hands and that tears were running down his cheeks.

Then Sir Percival, a young knight, rose to his feet. "We've glimpsed a miracle," he said. "I vow to you all, I will go on a quest to find the Grail and hold it in my hands. I will see it unveiled before I die, I swear it."

Then Sir Gawain got up and swore the same, and Sir Bors, and Sir Lancelot and Sir Galahad too. All the knights in the hall rose to their feet and swore to find the Holy Grail.

As he listened, Arthur had never been more proud of his knights' bravery. But he wanted to weep, for he knew that this would be the last time all his knights would feast together at Camelot. Merlin had told him that many knights would die upon the quest for the Holy Grail. However, all he said was: "In the morning. Tonight, let us eat, drink and be merry!"

Sitting beside Arthur, Guinevere looked to Lancelot, silently pleading with him to stay behind. But Lancelot quietly shook his head. His love for the queen was stronger than ever. But he was determined to follow the Grail.

At dawn the next day, the knights took leave of Arthur and Guinevere and set out on their quest for the Grail. They all went different ways, wishing one another well as they parted.

Lancelot rode for many weeks, through lonely valleys and desolate lands. One evening, he came across a dark, tangled forest and had to dismount and explore on foot.

"A chapel," he said, peering through the leaves. "Perhaps the Grail will be inside? It will surely be in a holy place."

But when he drew closer he found that all the doors were locked. And so, weary from his journey, he lay down and shut his eyes.

As he rested, half asleep and half awake, he saw a strange sight. A sick knight was being carried towards him by two servants. Then the door to the chapel opened and a hermit came out. He stood in prayer before the sick man, and then the Holy Grail appeared in the air, shining with such a bright, pure light that the full moon seemed dim.

"Please, let me drink," whispered the sick knight. "I wish to be healed."

The hermit raised the cup to the knight's lips and he drank. "I am well once more!" he declared. "Thanks be to God for this cure."

Then Lancelot longed to taste the liquid in that cup. "Please let me drink!" he cried.

But a voice said, "No, Lancelot. You stink of sin and you taste of death. You are not worthy."

Then the sick man rode away on Lancelot's horse and the hermit went once more into the chapel. As the door closed, Lancelot sat bolt upright, suddenly awake, not knowing if what he had seen was real or a dream. But when he found his horse was missing, he sank to the ground, sobbing. He knew now that he'd never find the Grail himself. He sobbed until he heard a noise and looked up to find the hermit beside him.

"I have done such wrong!" Lancelot blurted out. And he told the hermit of his love for Guinevere.

"You must leave all that behind now," said the hermit. "My name is Naciens. If you come with me, I will teach you, and help you to start anew."

So Lancelot stayed with Naciens for many

days before riding back to Camelot.

While Lancelot was at the chapel, Sir Percival had been riding along a dusty road. He hadn't seen a soul for days and when he heard the thunder of hooves, he felt cheered. "Perhaps these riders will be able to direct me on my quest?" he thought.

But as the knights came closer, he realized they had no intention of helping him.

"Chaaaaarge!" one cried.

"Kill him!" cried another.

"Never!" Percival cried back. He raised his lance and charged to meet them. With a mighty thrust, he pierced the first rider through the heart. He fell dead from his horse's saddle. But the rider second struck with a terrible blow, and Percival's horse was killed beneath him.

As his horse fell, Percival tumbled to the ground, and the blows kept coming, raining down from all sides. Percival fought back, but he was outnumbered. Soon, a strike would hit home and that would be the end of him.

"Get away from him!" a voice rang out. It was a young voice. A boy's.

Percival heard charging hooves and cries, and the sound of steel clashing on steel. Then someone was helping him up. It was a boy in red armour, panting for breath but without a scratch on him. All the knights who had attacked Percival lay dead around them. The boy raised his vizor. It was Sir Galahad.

"Thank y—" Percival began. But Sir Galahad was already leaping back onto his horse and thundering away.

As Percival struggled to his feet, he tore off his helmet and flung it to the ground. "I'm a knight. I shouldn't need to be rescued by a mere boy," he thought. He felt bitter humiliation flushing his face.

"Percival," came a voice. He turned, and saw a beautiful woman behind him. "Why are you scowling, Percival?" she asked gently.

"I'm angry," said Sir Percival. He couldn't meet her eye. "I'm angry with Sir Galahad."

The woman smiled at him with such kindness that his heart lifted. "Sir Galahad saved your life. There is no shame in needing help. But jealousy clouds your heart and keeps you from the Grail."

Percival blushed, feeling the truth of her words. "I swear, I will no longer envy Sir Galahad," he replied. "Instead, I will follow him, for surely he's the man who's worthy enough to find the Grail."

The lady smiled. "Then I know a faster way to find him." And from behind her appeared a great black horse, the most mighty steed Percival had ever seen. He swung up into the saddle, struck his spurs and the beast bounded away.

It charged through the forest, so fast that the world became a blur and Percival's eyes streamed. It leaped across walls, across rivers, through valleys and forests, and only stopped when they came to a deserted, stony shore.

Ahead of Percival, the grey sea stretched away, and it seemed as if he had come to the end of the world. But as he looked out across the waves, he saw a ship gliding towards him, without anyone on board. "Go now," a voice seemed to whisper. So Percival leaped into the ship and it carried him away...

Meanwhile, Sir Galahad had been travelling for many days, through barren and wasted lands, when he saw a black castle up ahead. He reined in his horse and stopped by an old man. "Sir, can you tell me the name of that castle?" he asked.

The old man scowled and spat. "That's the Castle of Maidens. Any knight who goes there is butchered. I'd turn back now if I were you."

"Why does anyone go near it?" asked
Sir Galahad.

"They say that all the maidens of the castle
are held prisoner by a wicked band of knights."
The old man squinted up at him. "Foolish boys
seem to think they can free them."

"Thank you for the warning," said Galahad.
"But I can't leave those women imprisoned by a
gang of scoundrels. I must go to their aid, even if
it takes me from my quest for the Holy Grail."

"Very well. It's your own grave you're
digging," the old man said, and went on his way.

As Galahad rode closer to the castle walls, he
saw that the fields all around it were full of dead
bodies. But that did not deter him. At the gate
he stopped and shouted up, "Let me in. I wish to

speak to the master."

A porter looked down through a window and laughed at him. "We'll show you who's master, little boy!"

With a crunching of gears, the portcullis rose and seven huge armoured knights rode out, all brandishing spears.

"Are you going to take me all at once, cowards?" cried Sir Galahad.

"We are," said the first knight. He charged, flanked by the other knights.

Sir Galahad had just enough time to raise his shield against the first assault. His horse reared, kicking the first knight from his horse. The knight fell dead to the ground.

As Galahad raised his sword, it began to glow. He swung it in a mighty arc and two more knights fell from their horses.

The others charged at him with shouts of fury. "Die! Die!" they cried. But Galahad sat firm in his saddle. His glowing blade sliced through the air and shattered a knight's shield. Again he swung, and again. Soon, the knights realized that they were beaten. They ran and staggered away as fast as they could, without a backward glance.

When the last knight had fled, Sir Galahad jumped from his horse. He saw a crowd of maidens hurrying across the drawbridge to greet him. They pressed him to accept gifts of thanks. But he shook his head. "It was my duty as a knight to free you," he said. "But I must not stay. I cannot rest until I find the Holy Grail."

"Then at least you won't go on alone," came a voice from behind him. He turned in the saddle to see Sir Percival. The older man was smiling at him. "It seems I owe you my life," he said. "And I know that if any man can reach the Grail, you are that man."

Sir Galahad returned his smile. "With a brother knight at my side, perhaps I can."

The two knights travelled side by side for many days. They rode high and low, facing many a challenge. The days turned into months and the months into years. Sir Galahad turned into a grown man and Sir Percival turned grey, his face a map of lines.

They searched every inch of the kingdom until one day they came to a forest in which every tree was dead. Sir Percival groaned. "This must be an omen. Perhaps we'll never find the Grail. It's time for us to return home."

But Sir Galahad shook his head. "God will show us the way."

No sooner had he said those words than he caught sight of an old man wandering between the trees. The old man looked up at Galahad. "Is it really you?" he croaked, his eyes bright with joy. "I have wandered many years to find you and tell you your mission. Now I've found you!"

"Naciens?" cried Galahad. "My dearest Naciens!" He clasped the old man's hand, and Nacien's squeezed it feebly.

"Go to the king," he whispered.

"Which king? Arthur?"

Naciens shook his head. "In the castle beyond

the river, King Pelles is badly wounded and has long been so. Go! Heal him!"

Sir Galahad felt tears prick at his eyes. "I cannot leave you like this," he said. He lifted Naciens gently onto his horse, and he and Sir Percival rode on across the river to the castle that lay beyond.

When they arrived, they were welcomed by solemn guards and taken to a gloomy chamber. Its walls were draped with silken hangings that had once been beautiful, but were now faded and pale. In the middle of the room, Galahad made out the shape of a man lying on a bed. It was the king, and he looked very close to death. "Come closer," he rasped.

Sir Galahad approached, with Sir Percival a few steps behind. The king looked Galahad straight in the eye. "I was wounded by a knight of King Arthur. Have you come to heal me of my wound?"

Sir Galahad said, "I'm only a knight, not a healer. How can I?"

The king smiled. "You are not only a knight. You are the best knight that there has ever been. Otherwise you would not carry that sword."

Then there was a flash of burning white light. All but Galahad had to shield their eyes. With a series of echoing slams, every window and door in the castle closed. Sir Galahad saw a group of glowing, ghostly maidens approaching him and the wounded king.

One of the maidens carried a shining cup. It was a simple shape, without ornament or carving. But from its pure and holy light, Sir

Galahad knew at once that this was the Grail —
the cup that he had only glimpsed at Camelot
beneath a veil.

The maidens walked slowly and solemnly. All
eyes were on them now. Galahad blinked. They
appeared to be fading as they moved past him.

"This must just be another glimpse," Percival
murmured. "Our quest is not done yet."

But Sir Galahad felt his soul leap and he knew
that Percival was wrong. He raised his sword and
cried out, "Stop!"

His sword began to glow like the Grail itself.
The procession slowed and the maidens turned
and brought the Holy Grail towards Sir Galahad.
The maiden who carried it held the cup out to
him, offering him a drink.

Sir Galahad took the cup and knelt beside the

'The maidens turned and brought the Holy Grail towards Sir Galahad.'

wounded king. "Drink this," he said, putting the cup to the man's lips. King Pelles drank deeply. As he drank, his wound began to heal and the flush of health and life returned to his face.

Sir Galahad then took the cup himself and drank too. "My quest is done," he said. "Now, I will go to God."

The Grail in his hands glowed brighter. Percival gasped as a winged figure swooped down and took Sir Galahad's hand. It carried Sir Galahad up and out of sight. Neither Sir Galahad nor the Grail would ever be seen on Earth again.

As Sir Percival left Castle Carbonek, he saw that the wasted lands around the castle had been restored. Grass grew and flowers bloomed where the ground had been barren before.

Straight away he rode to King Arthur, and

told him all that had happened, and Arthur held a great feast to celebrate. But so many knights had died in search of the Holy Grail that there was no true joy in his heart.

Still, he raised his cup to Galahad, and Lancelot joined in the toast. His heart swelled with pride at the thought of his son, and yet he felt a deep sadness within him. "I have failed," he thought. "My son is great, but I am an unworthy knight." And as he looked up, his eyes met Guinevere's.

Arthur followed Lancelot's gaze and shuddered. He knew that his wife would never truly be his, and that his best friend had stolen her heart. Then he looked around at all the empty places of the fallen knights. The dream of Camelot was ending.

The Strife Begins

I t was the merry month of May, when
the fields were bright with flowers.
But this May was like no other, for there
was anger and spite at the heart of
Camelot. Just as Merlin had foretold,
the shining days of the Round Table
were nearing their end...

Sir Agravain, Gawain's brother, had always been jealous of Lancelot's fame. For a long time, he had brooded on ways of hurting him. He had heard whispered rumours of the love between Lancelot and Guinevere, but he never had any proof, until one particular spring evening. He was walking in the castle gardens, when he overheard the couple talking privately.

Agravain hid behind a tree and watched, unseen, as Lancelot took Guinevere in his arms and kissed her.

Agravain rushed to his cousin, Sir Mordred, and told him what he had seen. Mordred's eyes gleamed darkly as he heard the tale. He knew that with this he could not only destroy Lancelot, he could break the fellowship of the Round Table.

Sir Mordred was Morgan Le Fay's son. His mother had brought him up to hate Arthur, and his deepest desire was to destroy Camelot. At last his chance had arrived.

That night, many of Arthur's knights were gathered in the Great Hall, when Agravain spoke up. "I marvel that we do so much to hide the truth," he said. "We all know that Lancelot loves Guinevere, and she loves him. They have betrayed the king. But no one does a thing about it!"

"Without Lancelot we would be mourning our king and queen. Lancelot has rescued them both many times," said Gawain. "Let us not speak of such things."

"I will not let this rest," said Mordred. "We must tell the king!"

"Does Lancelot's kindness and bravery mean nothing to you?" Gawain asked. "If Lancelot had not been here, we would all be worse off. Sir Agravain, did Lancelot not save you from Sir Tarquin's dungeon? Sir Mordred, has not Lancelot saved your life many times?"

He broke off as Arthur strode into the room. "No more of this now," Gawain muttered.

"We will speak!" Mordred hissed.

"In that case," said Gawain, "I will hear no more." He left, and his brothers Gaheris and Gareth followed him.

"What is all this muttering?" Arthur asked to the assembled knights.

"Sire," said Agravain, "I can keep this from you no longer. Mordred and I are sure Lancelot has committed treason. He loves your wife, and she loves him in return."

Arthur's face revealed nothing about his feelings. "Woe to you if this is a false rumour," he said grimly. "I would not call Lancelot a traitor unless I had proof."

"My Lord," said Sir Agravain, "we shall indeed bring you proof. Tomorrow morning you shall ride out hunting and Sir Lancelot will go with you. When night draws in, send word that you will stay away from the castle until the next day. That night we will catch Lancelot in the queen's chamber and we will bring him to you, dead or alive."

Arthur looked at Agravain. He sighed, then said, "Take twelve knights of the Round Table and do what must be done."

So Sir Mordred and Sir Agravain went to

choose the knights to accompany them. And Arthur sat alone in the Great Hall, with tears running down his face. For he knew, deep in his heart, that the accusations were true.

That evening, Sir Lancelot told his cousin Sir Bors that he was planning to visit the queen in her chambers.

"Do not go tonight, I beg you," Sir Bors replied. "You know how Sir Agravain and Sir Mordred watch every day to bring your downfall. Tonight, I fear there is some plan to trap you."

"Nonsense," said Sir Lancelot. "I have promised the queen I will visit her, and I will."

Sir Bors clasped Lancelot's hand. "I fear that if you visit her tonight, darkness shall come to us all."

"I am not a coward, Sir Bors," Lancelot said.

"Then I will pray that you come back safe and sound," Sir Bors replied.

That night, Lancelot went to the queen's chamber. Moments later, there was a pounding at the door. "Traitor knight, Sir Lancelot! Now you are taken!"

Lancelot recognized the voice of Sir Mordred. "Madam," he whispered, "is there any armour in here, that I might use as a shield? If there is anything, give it to me and they shall soon regret their malice."

"I have nothing," Guinevere replied.

"How many knights are outside the door? Ten? More? They will be armed. You cannot fight them all."

Her hands began to shake and tears slid down her cheeks. "You shall be killed, and I shall be taken."

"In all my life, I was never beaten," said Lancelot. "That I should be shamefully killed, for the lack of armour!"

"Traitor knight!" Sir Mordred thundered. "Come out of the chamber! You know you are surrounded!"

"I cannot bear this noise," said Lancelot. "Death would be better than this."

He took Guinevere in his arms and kissed her. "Most noble queen, as you have ever been my lady and I, at all times, have been your true knight, pray for my soul if I am killed. I am sure that Sir Bors will not fail to rescue you. Whatever happens to me, you shall be safe."

"I wish that they would kill me and let you escape," said Guinevere.

"That shall never be," said Lancelot. "God save me from such a shame!"

He kissed her once more, wrapped his mantle around him, and opened the door. Sir Gryflet burst through swinging his sword at Lancelot. Lancelot slammed the sword aside with his bare

arm and struck him with such a blow that he fell dead to the floor. Lancelot slammed the door shut once more.

'Lancelot opened the door and the knights came tumbling through it.'

Quickly, he dressed in the dead knight's armour. Outside the door, the knights were shouting louder than ever. "Traitor knight! Traitor knight!" they roared.

"Fair lords," he cried. "Leave off your shouting. You know well, Sir Agravain, that you shall not trap me tonight. I vow to you, by my knighthood, if you leave now, I shall appear before the king. And then I will answer you as a knight should. I will tell you that I have nothing to hide. I will prove it with my own hands."

"Traitor!" Sir Agravain shouted. "We'll mangle your brains."

"So, you have no mercy," Lancelot said softly. "Then be ready to fight and to die!"

Lancelot opened the door and the knights came tumbling through it. In the first moment,

Lancelot killed Sir Agravain. He struck again and again, and the twelve men who came after him were all soon cold on the floor. Only Sir Mordred was still alive. He ran from the scene, badly wounded.

"Madam," Lancelot whispered, "you know that from this moment, King Arthur will always be my enemy. Come with me and I will keep you from danger."

"That is not the right way," said Guinevere. "Go now. But do not forget me."

"Do not doubt me," said Lancelot. "While I still live, I will be true to you."

He kissed her, and then fled.

Lancelot went straight to Sir Bors and told him all that had happened. "You must summon your men," said Sir Bors. "War is upon us."

So, in the early light of dawn, Lancelot stood before a gathering of knights, all armed, ready to serve him. "I have killed Sir Agravain and twelve other knights," Lancelot said. "Now there will be a deadly war between me and Arthur. Guinevere was a faithful wife to her king. But now she will die for treason. I cannot allow that to happen. My lords, what will you do?"

"We will do as you do," Sir Bors replied, and the rest murmured their agreement.

"And what must I do, if Arthur puts Guinevere to death at the stake?"

"You must rescue her, as you have done many times before," said Sir Bors. "She is in peril for your sake, and you must save her."

And so Lancelot took his followers to a hidden place in the forest and made ready to rescue Guinevere.

At the same time, Sir Mordred came to Arthur as he sat talking to Gawain. When Arthur saw Mordred's ashen face and wounded arm, he knew what had happened.

"You took him in the queen's chamber?" said Arthur.

"We did," Mordred replied, and he told him all that had taken place.

"Then the fellowship of the Round Table is broken forever," Arthur said sorrowfully. "Many a noble knight will stand with Lancelot."

"And what of the queen?" said Mordred. "She has committed treason. And the punishment for treason is death by fire."

"Let us not rush to judge the queen," said Gawain hastily. "Lancelot was found in the queen's chamber. But it could be that he was there for no evil reason. Sometimes we do things for the best and it turns out for the worst. I am sure Guinevere is true. As for Lancelot, it is no surprise that he fought against knights who sought to trap him."

Arthur turned to Gawain. "Twelve of my knights lie dead!" he roared. Then he quietened and stared into the distance. For a moment, he looked lost. "My wife has committed treason and she shall have the law," he said quietly. "And if Lancelot ever returns to Camelot, he shall die a shameful death."

"I hope I never see it," said Gawain.

"How can you say that?" Arthur protested. "Last night Lancelot slew your brother Agravain and many other brave knights. You do not wish Lancelot's death?"

"I warned them not to fight him," Gawain said simply. "I am sorry for their deaths, but I did all I could to save them."

"Sir Gawain," said Arthur, "put on your armour. Bring Guinevere to the fire, where she will be judged and sentenced to death."

"I cannot do it," said Gawain.

"Then your brothers, Sir Gareth and Sir Gaheris, will do it."

And though Gawain begged him not to, Arthur sent for Sir Gaheris and Sir Gareth, and told them of their grim task.

"If we must go," said Gaheris, "we will be there in peace and not in war."

"Go!" Arthur boomed.

Within hours, Arthur's knights had built the stake. Gareth and Gaheris were among the knights who began to lead Guinevere slowly towards it. There were many who could not look as the queen was tied to the stake.

'...bright flames began to lick the air around Guinevere.'

A knight held a burning torch to the stake, and bright flames began to lick the air around Guinevere.

At that moment, Lancelot and his men broke cover and came galloping across the field. The field became a frenzy of swords and men, and in the mad heat of battle, Lancelot struck down Sir Gaheris and Sir Gareth.

When Lancelot had cut a path through his opponents, he rode up to the stake, sliced through the ropes that bound Guinevere, and galloped away with her on his horse.

They rode all day. That night, they arrived at Lancelot's castle, Joyous Garde. Many knights there pledged their allegiance to Guinevere and hoped that peace might be made between Lancelot and Arthur. Others said that nothing but woe and warfare was to come...

As the men returned from the battlefield, Gawain was watching and waiting. "Where are my brothers? I do not see them," he asked a young, wounded knight.

"Then you do not know," the knight replied sadly. "Sire, Gareth and Gaheris are dead."

All the blood drained from Gawain's face. "What are you telling me?"

"They are dead," the young man repeated.

"Who killed them?"

"Lancelot, Sire," replied the knight.

"Impossible," said Gawain. "Gareth loved Lancelot more than any man on Earth."

"Sire, it is widely known. Lancelot killed your brothers," the knight said.

Gawain staggered backwards and fainted to

the ground.

That night, Gawain burst through the doors
of the Great Hall, where Arthur sat lost in
thought. Privately, Arthur regretted more than
anything sending Guinevere to the stake. He had
wept with relief to hear that her life had been
saved. But the death of so many of his knights
made him numb with shock.

"My brothers are dead!" Gawain roared.

"It cannot be," said Arthur, shaking his head.
He could not believe it. "They were not armed."

"And yet Lancelot killed them," said Gawain,
in a trembling voice. "And by the ties that bind
us, I swear that I will not rest until I have
wreaked vengeance on Lancelot. I will kill him or
he will kill me. That is the sum of it. If I have to
seek him through seven kingdoms—"

"You will not need to," Arthur replied. "He is at his castle, Joyous Garde."

"Then I beg you, make war against Lancelot. Avenge my brothers' deaths. Rescue your queen and make peace with her," Gawain pleaded. Then he stormed from the hall, weeping for his brothers, while Arthur sat alone. And in the shadows behind him, Mordred stood, unseen, with a cruel, satisfied smile on his face.

The next morning, Arthur summoned all the best warriors in England to his side and rode to Joyous Garde. For fifteen weeks, his army laid siege to Lancelot's castle. But they could not break its defences.

One morning, Lancelot appeared on the battlements. "My lords, this siege will fail," he shouted. "If I fought, I would defeat you easily."

"Try me then!" Arthur cried. "I am waiting for you."

"God forbid that I should ever fight with the noble king who made me a knight."

"Your words are like so much air," said Arthur scornfully. "I am your mortal foe. And I will be so until the day I die. You killed my knights. You stole my queen."

Then Lancelot begged King Arthur to make peace. He offered to give up Guinevere and to defend her innocence, but Arthur would not listen. And so, the next morning, Lancelot led his men out of the castle and a terrible battle began.

Gawain searched for Lancelot, hoping to kill him, but in the confusion of the battle he killed Lancelot's cousin Sir Lionel instead.

Sir Bors struck Arthur with such a mighty

blow that he fell from his horse. Sir Bors stood over him, with his sword drawn. "Lancelot," he shouted, "shall I end this war with one stroke?"

"Do not strike him!" Lancelot thundered back. "Or I will slay you myself. I will not see any harm come to Arthur."

Then Sir Lancelot jumped down from his horse and helped Arthur back into his saddle. "Take back your queen and end this war, I beg you," Lancelot said to him. "If you do, I promise I will leave this kingdom and never return, unless you have need of me."

Arthur thought of all the times that Lancelot had come to his aid. And so he nodded, and a truce was agreed. That afternoon, Lancelot welcomed Arthur into his castle and led Guinevere before him.

"Most noble lord, I bring you your queen. If there is any knight who says she was false to you, I will fight him to the death. For you have listened to liars and those who seek to break the fellowship of the Round Table."

As he said these words, Lancelot looked over at Mordred, whose face flushed scarlet.

"The king can do what he likes," Gawain interrupted. "You killed my brothers and I will never make peace with you."

"You know that I loved no man more than Sir Gareth," said Lancelot.

"I know that I will never forgive you," Gawain replied.

"I bid you farewell," Lancelot said to Arthur. "I shall leave at once for France."

"Be sure that I will find you there," said

Gawain. "For if you go to the ends of the Earth, you will never escape me."

For a time, peace ruled in the kingdom, but it was an uneasy peace, for Gawain still brooded on the deaths of his brothers. He urged Arthur to go to war against Lancelot and so did Sir Mordred. Before many months had passed, hundreds of knights joined with Gawain – and Arthur reluctantly declared war on Lancelot.

So Arthur led his army to fight him in France. And since Mordred was his sister's son, and had lately been by his side, always ready with advice, Arthur left Mordred to rule in his place while he was away.

In France, Arthur marched to the great castle where Lancelot was staying and laid siege to it. Every day Gawain stood outside the castle, challenging Lancelot to fight him, until, with a heavy heart, Lancelot finally agreed. They fought each other three times, and each time Lancelot struck Gawain with a terrible blow to the head. Each time he could have killed him, but instead he walked away.

And then it seemed as if Gawain was mad, for as he lay bleeding on the ground, he cried out: "Slay me! For when I am recovered, I will fight you again. I will not rest until one of us is dead."

Through the long, cold winter, the siege continued.

Meanwhile, in Camelot, many of the younger knights began to see Mordred as their leader. And now he realized that not only could he destroy Arthur and the Round Table, he could seize the throne for himself...

The Last Battle

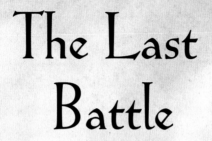

W hile Arthur was fighting in France, Mordred plotted against him. One day he announced that Arthur had been killed in battle. "Our king is dead. As his heir, I will do all I can to follow in his footsteps," he declared.

He was crowned in the cathedral, surrounded by people who wept for Arthur. Afterwards, Mordred went to see Guinevere. "As your husband is dead and I am now king, it is proper that you marry me," he told her.

Guinevere was so shocked, she hardly knew how to reply. She was sure he was lying about Arthur's death. Somehow she felt certain that Arthur was still alive. But she returned Mordred's smile. "I will obey you in all things," she said sweetly. Privately, she began to plot her escape, gathering support from knights she trusted with her life.

The next week, she told Mordred she was going to London to make arrangements for their wedding. Once she arrived, she locked herself in the Tower of London. Her trusted knights

surrounded the tower to protect her, and she
sent a message to Arthur, begging him to return.

When Mordred heard she had escaped, he was
wild with rage. He rushed to the tower. "I am
your king," he shouted. "You will marry me or
spend the rest of your life imprisoned here!"

Guinevere prayed for Arthur's return. For
weeks she heard nothing. Then, one day, a
messenger brought news: Arthur was on
his way.

The news reached Mordred too and that night
his army marched south to greet Arthur's
returning ships. By dawn, he was on the cliffs,
watching Arthur's ships as they swept in from
the sea.

He was certain his army would be more than
a match for Arthur. So he watched without a

shred of fear as the ships landed on the beach and
knights streamed out of them.

Among them was Arthur, who leaped from
his ship, hurtling straight into the fray. He
fought Mordred's knights like a fearless lion,
inspiring his knights to fight harder than they
ever had before. The beach became a whirlwind
of swords. Men fought on the beach, in the sea,
on the ships.

Mordred watched, smiling, from the clifftop while his knights fought below. But his smile soon faded as he realized that Arthur's knights were crushing his men.

"Away! We must away!" Mordred shouted. He set his spurs to his horse and fled, and his men went racing after him.

When the battle was over, Arthur found Sir Gawain, lying half dead on the deck of a ship. He took him tenderly in his arms.

"Alas, good Gawain," he said, "you are leaving me, and all my joy is gone. You and Lancelot were the two knights I loved best in the world. Soon I will have lost you both."

"My death is coming, it is true," Gawain said with a sigh. "But it is my own fault. I wanted revenge, and what did it bring? I will lose my own life, and you have lost Lancelot's friendship forever. Please, bring me pen and paper. I must write to Lancelot before it is too late."

So the paper was brought and Gawain struggled to write, in a shaky hand:

Lancelot, I wish to tell you that today, on the 10th of May, I was struck in the same place that you wounded me. Soon I will be dead. Outside the walls of your castle, you hit me with

a deadly blow. But my death is not your fault.
I have been killed by my own pride. Forgive me,
I beg you. Come, noble Lancelot, for the realm is
in peril. Today we put the traitor Mordred to
flight. Come swiftly, before Mordred can gather
fresh rebels.

Noble Lancelot, farewell.

Then Gawain died, and Arthur spent the long
night weeping by his side.

The next day brought another bloody battle
against Mordred. Then Mordred fled west, and
Arthur marched with his men to Cornwall, to
fight him once more.

The night before the battle, Arthur dreamed
that he was sitting on his throne, dressed in a
golden cloak.

The throne was lashed to a wooden wheel and beneath him was a pool of black water, filled with writhing serpents. Suddenly the wheel jerked forwards, and he was thrown into the water. Arthur let out a terrible cry – and awoke.

After that, unable to sleep, he left his tent and paced in the field outside. And as the sun rose, he saw a strange thing. For suddenly Gawain appeared in front of him, accompanied by many fair ladies.

"My dearest nephew," Arthur said.

"My dearest king," Gawain replied, "Each of these women I fought for while I lived. Through God's mercy, He has allowed them to bring me here, to warn you of your death. For if you fight Mordred tomorrow, you shall both fall and many of your knights with you. What you must do is this: sign a treaty for a month. Then Lancelot and his knights will come to your aid, and together you will vanquish your enemies."

The vision faded and Arthur found himself looking at the field before him, the wind moving through the grass and a single crow sitting on a bare branch.

He hurried back through the field, called for his knights, and told them of the vision. "Go to Mordred's camp straight away," he ordered Sir

Lucan and his brother, Sir Bedevere. "Beg them
to keep the peace for one month. Spare nothing
to persuade them. Give them lands and treasure,
whatever they ask for."

So the knights rode to Sir Mordred. They
talked for a long time and promised him the
lands of Kent and Cornwall. Finally, Mordred
agreed to keep the peace. To cement the truce,
the two men would meet with their armies the
next day and exchange a kiss of peace.

"That is good news indeed," said Arthur,
when his knights returned. "But if any of you see
one of Mordred's men raise his sword, then
attack him at once. For I do not trust that man."

At the same time, Mordred told his followers
the same thing. "If you see one of Arthur's
soldiers reach for his sword, kill as many of his

men as you can, for I do not trust Arthur."

The next day, the two men met. Both men signed the truce. They kissed, and then drank from the same cup as a sign of peace.

As they were doing this, an adder slid from under a bush and bit one of Mordred's knights on the heel. Without thinking, the knight drew his sword and killed it.

One of Arthur's men saw the drawn sword and lunged. The next moment, the field had erupted into a storm of clashing swords. There had never been a more terrible battle.

It raged all the day, until one hundred thousand knights lay dead on the cold ground.

When the fighting was over, Arthur looked

over the battlefield, half mad with grief. Nearly all his knights were dead. He could only see two still living – the brothers Sir Lucan and Sir Bedevere, both badly wounded.

"I wish I had never seen this day," Arthur said. "But where is Mordred, the maker of all of this mischief?"

He looked across the field and saw Mordred alone, leaning on his sword. "Give me your spear," Arthur said grimly to Sir Lucan.

Sir Lucan begged him to leave Mordred. "We have won the battle," Lucan said. "There are three of us, but Mordred is alone. If you fight him, you will both die!"

"Give me my spear!" Arthur thundered. "Whether I live or die, I will take revenge on the man who has destroyed the kingdom."

'...Arthur strode through the battlefield.
With a terrible cry, he rushed at Mordred and struck him.'

So Lucan gave Arthur the spear, and Arthur strode through the battlefield. With a terrible cry, he rushed at Mordred and struck him. Mordred cried out and staggered backwards, before he found his footing and swung at Arthur with all his strength.

His sword smashed across Arthur's head and cracked his skull. Then Mordred dropped his sword, stumbled, and fell dead to the ground.

As Sir Lucan and Sir Bedevere rushed to Arthur's side, they found him lying quite still. He was barely alive.

Very carefully, they carried him to a chapel by the sea, where he could rest. Sir Lucan himself was sorely wounded and, after delivering his king to the chapel, he sank to the ground and died.

Bedevere wept over his brother, who he had loved dearly. Arthur reached out and laid a hand on his shoulder. "Do not weep, gentle knight. Tears will not help us now. Please take my sword, Excalibur, to the lake beyond the edge of the forest. Drop it into the water. Then come back and tell me what you saw."

So Bedevere rode away with Excalibur. But on the way to the lake, he looked at Excalibur, with all its shining jewels. It seemed like an act of madness to throw such a beautiful sword away. "Arthur is close to death. He does not know what he is saying. Why should I listen to the ramblings of a dying man?" Bedevere thought. And so he hid the sword under a bush and rode back to Arthur. "I threw the sword in the lake," he said.

"And what did you see?" asked Arthur.

"Nothing but the lake beneath the sky."

Arthur looked hard at his knight. "Why betray your king for the sake of a few jewels?" he asked. "Go back and follow my command."

Again Bedevere rode away. When he returned, Arthur asked him again, "What did you see?"

"The wind rippling the water," said Bedevere.

"You are still lying. Quickly, go and throw the sword into the lake. I do not have long."

Then, full of shame, Bedevere rode swiftly to the forest and flung the sword out across the dark waters of the lake.

As Excalibur flew through the air, night turned into day. The waters shone with a dazzling light, and a hand rose from the water and caught the sword.

'...a hand rose from the water and caught the sword.'

The hand waved the sword three times in the air and then sank. The light faded, and the lake was still once more.

Bedevere stood staring, barely able to believe what he had seen. When he returned to Arthur and told him what had happened, Arthur lay back. "Good," he said. "Now help me to my feet, for my time has come."

So Bedevere did as he asked and they slowly made their way down to the shore. Night had fallen. The sea was still and a thick, white mist floated over it.

As they waited, a ship appeared in the mist. As it came closer, Arthur saw many women, dressed in black, upon the deck. He recognized Lady Nimue, and frowned as he saw his sister, Morgan Le Fay. But his sister was quite changed.

All the hatred was gone from her face and she looked at her brother with love and sorrow.

Merlin's words, from so many years before, came back to Arthur: *She will be with you at the end, and her grasping heart will be washed of all its evil...*

"Help me, one last time," Arthur said to Bedevere. So Bedevere held out his arm, as Arthur climbed onto the boat. On the deck, Arthur lay down.

"Why did you wait so long?" Morgan whispered, kneeling beside him. "Your wounds are so deep."

He shut his eyes and felt the comfort of her hand on his shoulder. As if caught by a gentle tide of magic, the boat began to glide slowly away from the shore.

"Where are you going?" Sir Bedevere called.

"To the Vale of Avalon to rest and be healed,"
Arthur replied. "Be sure that I will come again
when my kingdom needs me. And then the
kingdom will rise out of darkness. If you do not
hear of me again, pray for my soul."

The boat was lost in the mist and all was
quiet, except for a strange sad sound, like the cry
of a bird, which echoed in the distance.

That night Bedevere wandered, weeping,

hardly knowing where he was going. All Arthur's knights were dead. The kingdom was lost, and now the king himself was gone. When the sun rose, he found himself at a hermitage. A priest was kneeling in prayer by a freshly dug grave.

"Father, who is buried here?" he asked.

"I do not know," said the old man. "Last night, some ladies brought a body here and gave me gold and candles to bury him."

Bedevere sank to his knees, knowing at once that he had found King Arthur's grave. He vowed to spend the rest of his life in the forest, praying beside his king.

Lancelot's Return

When Lancelot received Gawain's letter, he set out at once for England. But by the time he arrived, it was too late. Arthur and Mordred were both dead. Lancelot went to the tomb of his old friend Gawain.

He spent three days kneeling by the tomb, praying for the soul of the noble knight. Then he set out in search of Guinevere. He did not know where to find her – he had only heard that she had travelled west.

One day, he stopped by chance at an abbey in Amesbury. Lancelot did not know it, but when Guinevere heard that Arthur had died she had taken holy orders. As Guinevere caught sight of him walking in the grounds of the abbey, she fainted. When she opened her eyes, the other nuns were bending over her.

"Do not worry," she told them. "I am not unwell. I was merely surprised by the sight of the knight over there. Please, call him to me."

And so they called Lancelot into the cloister, and Guinevere spoke up in a cool, clear voice.

"Because of the love between me and this man, the most noble knights in the world were killed," she declared. "Because of us, my most noble lord and king died. Lancelot, I have come here to ask forgiveness for my sins. I can never see you again. Go home. Take a wife who will live with you happily. Pray for me, Lancelot."

For a moment Lancelot did not speak, though tears ran down his cheeks. "So I am to go home and find a wife? I could never do that. I could never be false to you. I will become a hermit and pray for you day and night."

"If you are able, Lancelot."

"If you can forsake the world, so can I," he replied. "But before I go, I must ask you one thing."

"What is it?" asked Guinevere.

"Good queen, grant me one last kiss."

"No, Lancelot, I cannot do that," said Guinevere, turning away.

So, without another word, Lancelot walked to his horse. As he rode away, he cried out as if he had been wounded and Guinevere fainted again to the ground.

Lancelot galloped through the countryside and he did not stop until he heard a bell ringing for mass. Following the noise, he came upon a chapel, half hidden between two cliffs. Beside it, he found Sir Bedevere and the hermit praying by a grave. He knew at once that he had found Arthur's resting place and he vowed to stay there for the rest of his life.

One night, he dreamed that Guinevere was dying, and that he should go and bury her body beside her husband. The following morning he set out for Amesbury. When he arrived, the abbess told him she had died half an hour before.

Lancelot and several men took her bier, lit with a hundred candles, to King Arthur's grave. There, Guinevere was buried next to Arthur.

Gazing at their graves, Lancelot knew that it was he who had caused their deaths. From that time on, he refused all food or drink. Within weeks, he was dead. But he died with a smile on his face, as if he had been surprised by happiness.

❧ ❧ ❧

That is all that is known of the life and death of Arthur and his knights. Some say that Arthur will return one day, when the kingdom needs him. When he does, Merlin will awaken from his long sleep under the earth, and together they will bring the land out of darkness.

But until that time, Arthur lies in his tomb, in a forgotten corner of a peaceful forest. And on his tombstone, these words are written:

HIC IACET ARTHURUS, REX QUONDAM REXQUE FUTURUS.

That is to say: here lies Arthur, the once and future King.

'...Arthur lies in his tomb, in a forgotten corner of a peaceful forest.'

The Story of a Legend

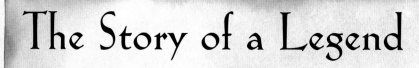

Stories of King Arthur have been around for centuries. So popular and so powerful are these tales that people feel they must be based on truth. And perhaps they are. But most of what we know of Arthur is from the stories, so it's difficult to tell which parts are fact.

In a *History of Britain* written in the 9th century by a Welsh monk called Nennius, Arthur was a warrior who won battle after battle against invaders. But there's no way one man could really have fought in all the battles listed – without the aid of magic.

In the 12th century, a historian called Geoffrey of Monmouth wrote about Arthur, his knights, Guinevere and Merlin in his *History of the Kings of Britain*. The work claimed to be factual but, checked against other historical sources, the 'facts' have turned out to be incorrect.

Around the same time, the legend was becoming popular in France. A poet, Chrétien de Troyes, wrote long poems about Arthur and his knights, adding new material including Lancelot's love for Guinevere, and the Grail.

Then in the 15th century an English knight, Thomas Malory, retold all the stories he could find about King Arthur in a book called *Le Morte D'Arthur* (The Death of Arthur). This was the most complete version yet. Most of the stories in this book are based on it.

The Characters of Legend

Since the legend has existed, characters have been added or altered with each retelling, usually to reflect the interests of the time. Here are a few of the most popular characters:

Arthurian Knights

Sir Lancelot - Most courageous knight who performs countless heroic deeds. Arthur's closest friend. In love with Guinevere, Arthur's wife. Father of Sir Galahad.

Sir Gawain - Very loyal, honourable knight. A brother to Agravain, Gareth and Gaheris. Takes on the Green Knight. Marries the hideous Lady Ragnell to save Arthur's life.

Sir Galahad - The purest knight in Arthur's kingdom. Sir Lancelot's son. Succeeds in the quest for the Holy Grail but never returns.

Sir Gareth - A brave but humble knight. Close friend of Sir Lancelot. Gawain's brother. Nicknamed 'Sir Lovely Hands' by Sir Kay before he reveals his identity.

Sir Kay - Arthur was brought up as Kay's younger brother. Arrogant, boastful but basically loyal knight.

Sir Percival - A pure, brave knight. His father and brothers were knights and died young. His mother brought him up in a forest to stop him suffering the same fate. After seeing knights riding by, he rushes off to become one. Later he helps Sir Galahad on the quest for the Holy Grail.

Sir Mordred - Arthur's jealous nephew. Son of Arthur's evil sister Morgan Le Fay, who plots against him.

Magical Characters

Merlin - A powerful wizard and advisor to
Arthur. He has a deep knowledge of magic
and can see into the future. Entombed alive
under a hill by his love, the enchantress
Lady Nimue.

Morgan Le Fay - Arthur's half-sister. She
uses magic to plot against him to bring
about the downfall of the kingdom.
Married to Sir Urien, and the mother
of Sir Uwain and Sir Mordred.

The Lady of the Lake - A mysterious
enchantress who gives Arthur his magic
sword, Excalibur. She is killed by Sir Balyn
under the influence of another magic sword
which can only do good in the hands of
Sir Galahad.

Lady Nimue - An enchantress who learns
magic from Merlin, entraps him with a
spell, and brings Sir Lancelot to Camelot.

The Green Knight - Mysterious knight who is green from top to toe. Challenges Arthur's knights to chop off his head and receive a blow from him in return. Gawain accepts the challenge and his courage, honesty and honour are tested.

Code of Chivalry

Throughout history, knights have been expected to follow certain rules of behaviour. These have became known as the Code of Chivalry. To the knights of the Round Table, this meant:

1. Never commit murder.

2. Never commit treason against the king.

3. Grant mercy to anyone who asks (even in battle).

4. Always go to the aid of ladies who need help.

5. Never harm women.

6. Only fight on behalf of a good cause.

Usborne Quicklinks

For links to websites to find out more about King Arthur,
go to www.usborne.com/quicklinks and type the title of this book.
We recommend that children are supervised while using the internet.

Additional writing by Louie Stowell
Edited by Anna Milbourne
Designed by Russell Punter

Digital manipulation by Nick Wakeford

First published in 2014 by Usborne Publishing Ltd., Usborne House,
83-85 Saffron Hill, London EC1N 8RT, England. www.usborne.com